T0058029

YOUNG MAN IN CHAINS

FRANÇOIS MAURIAC

YOUNG MAN IN CHAINS

(L'Enfant Chargé de Chaines)

Translated by
GERARD HOPKINS

FARRAR, STRAUS AND GIROUX

NEW YORK

L'Enfant Chargé de Chaines
was first published in 1913
This translation
Young Man in Chains
first published 1961
© 1961 *Eyre & Spottiswoode*
ISBN 0-374-52675-3

Printed in Great Britain

PUBLISHERS' NOTE

It was in December 1943, when France was still enemy-occupied territory, that the English publishers, at the instigation of Mr Graham Greene, who was then their editorial director, tried to acquire the translation rights of the novel which, it was rumoured, François Mauriac had recently published, *La Pharisienne*. The book could not be obtained in London but when, after the Liberation, communications with Paris became possible once more, it was decided to extend the original proposal and issue a collected edition in English of all Mauriac's novels, and to commission Mr Gerard Hopkins, well known for his translation of Jules Romains' monumental *Hommes de Bonne Volonté*, to do it. One or two of Mauriac's novels had been translated in England and America during the twenties and thirties without attracting much attention from the general reading public. Yet everyone interested in French literature recognized François Mauriac as the greatest of living French novelists.

La Pharisienne appeared in the English translation, *A Woman of the Pharisees*, in 1946. It was received most enthusiastically by a public which had been cut off from French contemporary writing for more than six years. The book, now in its fourth impression, was followed by *Thérèse* in 1947, which has also run into four impressions. Since then, titles have appeared regularly every year or so and the publishers have been deeply gratified because they have been able, through the public response, to carry their edition to completion with *L'Enfant chargé de chaines*, Mauriac's first novel, written between 1909 and 1912. The collected edition of Mauriac's novels thus represents half a century of creative writing by one of the few twentieth century masters of the novel.

I

JEAN-PAUL had taken a tiny fifth-floor flat in the rue de Bellechasse. The windows looked on to a landscape of roofs. His father had sent him some pieces of old furniture which had been lying forgotten in the attics of the family house in the country. They had been familiar with the circumscribed existence of his grandparents, and, like old retainers, meeting again after a long separation, recognized the young man as the child who, so often, had bumped his head against their corners. Among them was a clock which, in those days, used to wake Jean-Paul in a sleep-deadened bedroom surrounded by the terrifying country silence.

He spent his time in pursuing the humdrum routine of work imposed upon him by the course of lectures which he was attending at the Sorbonne, and in writing, for obscure magazines, poems about the value of which his mind was not altogether made up.

On his writing-table stood a photograph of the mother he had never known. She looked out at him with the tired smile of one already suffering from the ravages of a mortal ailment. His father, Bertrand Johanet, lived in Guyenne where he owned a farm surrounded by heath-land. No one killed more woodcock than he did in the winter months, and, in August, when the pine-woods scorched in the sun, he spent most of his time instructing the peasants when to light the protective fires which set a defensive wall against the all-devouring furnace.

He knew very little about his son, nor did Jean-Paul know

very much about the tanned, hirsute and untidy man who was his father. He would wonder at times what strange chance had so arranged matters that he should owe his life to this stranger. 'At my age,' he would think, 'his greatest pleasure was to set off at dawn with a wagonload of friends and a pack of dogs curled up on the floor-boards. . . . I am twenty, and the only thing which makes it possible for me to live is the happiness I find in examining myself by the light of what I find in the books I most adore. I often feel the need of music to express the trite sentimentalities of youth, and take pleasure, too, in fluttering round any human heart that comes my way, like one of the moths which fly about the lamp when, on summer evenings, the dining-room windows looking on to the garden, stand open.'

II

A DAY came when Jean-Paul looked at his room and realized how ugly it was. In the clear afternoon light the reproductions of pictures by Carrière and Maurice Denis showed up as chromo-lithographs. The corners of the Tanagra statuette in sham terra-cotta were chipped. Surrounded by these vulgarities, he felt as though a tide of muddy water were rising inside him, a profound sense of nausea. He set about tracing this to its source, and realized that his mediocrity had stood revealed in a conversation he had had with a better educated friend, and that a question put to him by one of the lecturers had humiliated him before a roomful of mannerless oafs.

He could not, therefore, find consolation in the thought that his fit of gloom was due to his own superiority of mind: it derived from entirely trivial causes. Struck by this discovery, he composed a sonnet which, at first, he thought was not wholly without merit. When, however, he read it through again, he was staggered by its flatness.

The bell of Saint-François-Xavier struck five. He decided to take a walk. On his way downstairs, he murmured: 'I am accomplishing nothing . . . I shall fail in my exam . . . I must really start drawing up a programme of work tomorrow. . . .' He had noticed, more than once, that the decision to draw up a programme of work invariably brought him peace of mind. He strolled along the rue de Rennes. He hated its shop-fronts spilling over on to the pavement, and its ecclesiastical outfitters.

The window of the Café Lavenue was brightly lit. There, he thought, he would take refuge and stupefy himself with the illustrated papers. Just as he was settling down with a small cup of chocolate, somebody called to him:

'Hullo, old man!'

He turned his head. Louis Faveau, a wretched little nobody, extended a flabby hand which felt damp to the touch.

He secretly rejoiced in the knowledge that he would find no difficulty in conversing with 'Lulu'—as the nobody was nick-named—and sat for a few moments listening to him . . . 'I'm all in, old man . . . one late night after another . . . and then, that girl of mine. . . .'

He proceeded to give a detailed and shocking description of the girl in question.

Jean-Paul was astonished to find that he was looking at his companion with a sort of dull anger, and a faint feeling of envy. 'He doesn't know what suffering means,' he told him-self: 'worldliness, love, the races, tennis, golf, cards, seem to provide him with sufficient reasons for being alive. It isn't that he treats such things as the "relaxations" which Pascal held them to be. He doesn't need to seek relaxation from a spiritual unease which never touches him.'

He gazed at the pasty face which the use of a monocle rendered still more imbecile, taking in its air of self-satisfied lassitude. It would be a great satisfaction, he felt, to punch it to pulp. But even in his insolence there was a quality of caution.

'I can't help wondering,' he said, 'how it is you don't get sick of such mild pleasures.'

'Mediocre?—ah! my boy, you don't know Liane!'

'If I were to have a fling, as you call it—I should do my best to make it something on a really grand scale. That would be my excuse. I should revel in the "sumptuous joys of Persia and the Popes" of which Verlaine speaks, when he conjures up a vision of satanic youths in palaces of silk and gold at Ecbatana. . . . I should picture forth a world of indescribable delights. . . .'

'You're pulling my leg,' said Lulu.

Ever since their schooldays he had felt baffled by Jean-Paul. The fellow was always too subtle for him, and he never knew how to deal with him. 'Ought I to pretend to understand what he's saying, or should I take a shot at being annoyed?' On this particular day he conveniently remembered an engagement, shook Jean-Paul's hand, and made himself scarce.

Once more alone, Jean-Paul savoured the delight of being no longer 'strung up'. The pavements were gleaming. A melancholy sense of peace hung above the roadway. His sense of gloom had become appreciably lighter. He forgot its trivial causes. He was painfully conscious of the uselessness of his life. There had been times when he had sketched a version of Rastignac's challenging gesture, and been tempted to fling in the face of Paris the other's 'Now it's just the two of us—the fight is on!' But his small failures, his lassitude, his feeling of disgust had driven him back to his room, there to take refuge from the bustle of the streets in books.

'Perhaps it is to books,' he reflected, 'that I owe my melancholy. What is the point in catching a distant glimpse of Paradise when I am too second-rate ever to reach it? . . . Yet, what is to become of me if I don't read?'

Each year, when July hung heavily upon the town, and the benches in the Public Gardens, when dusk began to fall, were peopled with shiny faces dulled in sleep, Jean-Paul, to whom his father had handed over the money which had been left him by his mother—an income of fifteen thousand francs*— travelled expensively.

*Then £600 a year.

But the new scenes through which he moved were powerless to console him.

'The little world which I carry within myself never changes' —he thought; 'besides, all cities look alike: electric trams running between shop-windows. Too much has been said about places, like Venice, which claim to be out of the ordinary. The impressions I take away with me are but memories of what I have read in D'Annunzio, Barrès and Henri de Régnier. . . .'

When the rains of Autumn came, he had always found his greatest pleasure in going to earth deep in the heathy solitudes which had formed the background to his childhood's games. With him present, his father never ventured on more than two glasses of Armagnac, talked about the market price of resin, and embarked on endless stories of the days he spent out shooting, while Jean-Paul, pretending to listen, was free to think of other things. The remote and lonely huts where, in October, men lay in wait to net wild pigeons, were, for his son, but a melancholy refuge.

'Must I go home?'—he wondered: 'or shall I look up some friends?'

He started off in the direction of the students' club in the rue du Luxembourg where he was always sure of finding a few companions who had the gift of listening when he talked, of smiling, of being convinced. He enjoyed watching them live their lives, giving them advice, acting as their director. He turned their feet from the primrose path by telling them of his own struggles of conscience, and of how, sometimes, he had succumbed to temptation. But, because he thought that his true history was insufficiently entertaining, he served it up artfully embellished for the benefit of his young friends. . . .

While, in a nearby Café, a violinist set the feelings of his pensive listeners vibrating, he would tell them, guardedly, of the orgies in which he had participated before his conversion, though, in his description of them, he had to fall back upon his recollection of des Esseintes' fantasies. Then, he would describe the conversion, utilizing for the purpose a certain *Nuit de Pascal*, a work composed in his younger days, which had been much praised by his masters.

In this circle of young Catholics, Jean-Paul turned theologian. He spiced his talk with a grain of modernism, waxed enthusiastic over immanence and interior revelation, absorbed, twenty minutes before dinner, a brief resumé of Kant's philosophy which allowed him to demonstrate, over the fruit, that St Thomas Aquinas was no longer enough. He spoke with irony of the Encyclical *Pascendi*, of the Jesuits, of the Cardinal-Secretary of State, declared that the time had come to revert to the great mystical tradition, and grew sentimental over St Francis of Assisi. . . . Then, followed by a small body of admirers, he would set out on a sightseeing trip of the Right Bank, and run aground in the Promenade of a Music-Hall.

But this small change of zealotry no longer amused him. To the society of these puerile and spineless spirits he now preferred a self-imposed loneliness.

By the time dusk fell, he was back in his room. The last of the daylight lay like fine ashes on the roof-tops. He did not light his lamp, but sat by the fireplace in the dark, seeking in the far distance of his past some vague memory of a love-affair, some recollection of a friendship, with which to soften the hard tyranny of isolation. Why did there come back into his mind the image of himself, at fourteen, in the third class,

of himself in the last year of his childhood? Each Sunday he
would ask out for the day one of the youngest boarders, whose
starved affections had found in him their only food, and
would drive him back to the school-house in the evening.

He remembered those late Sunday afternoons in Bordeaux,
the dust turned to gold by the setting sun, the crowds straggling
over the pavements.

'Is that the only sentimental episode my life can show?'—he
wondered.

He lit the lamp, and saw, reflected in the mirror, his weedy,
youthful figure which had grown too quickly, his brown and
melancholy eyes. He smiled, and, in a low voice, spoke the
name of her whom he did not love, but in whose love he was
wrapped: Marthe.

This young cousin, Marthe Balzon, lived in the rue Garancière with her father, Jules Balzon, who taught rhetoric in the
Lycée Montaigne. Though blessed with a considerable fortune,
Monsieur Balzon remained attached to the University, for he
liked teaching the young and cared little about promotion.
Castelnau, his property in the Gironde, abutted on the Johanet
estate, and there, each year, Marthe and Jean-Paul would renew
their friendship.

Their mothers had been fellow-pupils at the Sacré-Coeur in
Bordeaux. Marriage had done nothing to weaken the bonds
which had linked the two young girls who had walked together under the Convent plane-trees, and had set a small but
noticeable gap between them and their companions. In the
sluggish days and weeks of the Summer holidays, they left
their children in the charge of the same English nurse, and, in the
cool darkness of an old country drawing-room, would take
turns at reading *Indiana* aloud. In 1893 the heat in the low-
lying lands of Guyenne, where water is a dangerous breeding-

ground of sickness, was intense, and the two friends were carried off in the same month by a fever. . . .

Jean-Paul looked for a moment at the photograph of his mother, with the sad smile which he loved so well, then, thinking that he would go and see Marthe after dinner, tasted in anticipation the pleasure of touching with his lips a delicate face from which all colour had departed.

B

III

M ARTHE came towards him holding a lamp high. 'Can it be you, Jean-Paul? Your visits, dear cousin, are so very few and far between.'

She took his hand and led him into the room he knew so well.

A brass-bedstead stood in one corner, with, as coverlet, an old piece of appliqué-work. On the wall was a crucifix, and a number of statuettes, all carefully coloured: St Joseph, with a bald crown and a brown fringe; a Virgin in a robe of nougat-pink, the neatest of neat Sacred Hearts. On some standing shelves were ranged several books, bound in light blue and dark red—an *Imitation*, several of the *Christian Manuals* series, and other pious works, each with an inscription on the front page—*in memory of a happy day*. Photographs of naked babies, and of young girls wearing the smiles peculiar to photographic studios, stood on the mantelpiece.

'Still got the Aunt Sally show, I see,' said Jean-Paul, pointing to the collection of statuettes which had always exasperated him, . . . 'they make a mock of religion. Remember what Huysmans says. . . .'

'I don't know . . . I have never read him.'

'You've read nothing!' muttered Jean-Paul contemptuously . . .'

'And you've read too much. . . .'

She had taken up again the piece of embroidery which she had laid down when he arrived. The lamp made a tiny point of brightness on her gold thimble. She raised her limpid eyes and, fearing that she might have vexed him, smiled. . . . Jean-Paul looked at the tired mouth with its slightly drooping corners, the over-thin shoulders, the heavy coils of tawny hair, and suddenly felt that he longed to bury his face again in the folds of her dark-coloured dress, as on a distant evening he had done.

'Why do you say that I have read too much, Marthe?'

'Because, dear cousin, your reading makes you unhappy. Perhaps I do not understand your melancholy moods and your complexities, but I do know what causes them. . . .'

'Do not try to understand. . . .'

'Oh! I am well aware that you are better educated than I am, more intelligent. But I cannot help feeling that you are the victim of your reading, that you take books too seriously. . . .'

'You're a little silly. . . .'

'I am not an intellectual, if that is what you mean . . . but I enjoy reading, all the same. . . . Only, you see, when I have finished a book I forget all about it: I don't make it part of my life. Zette, my little twelve-year-old cousin, is always asking me to lend her books by Zénaïde Fleuriot, because they make her cry, and she likes crying, she says. But when she has enjoyed her little cry she wipes her eyes and plays with her doll—which is just as it should be. . . .'

Jean-Paul got up.

'You'll never understand me,'—he murmured.

She looked at him with swimming eyes, her hands crossed on the dark stuff of her dress, and they spoke of indifferent matters. No, her father was not in. She was going to a matinée at the Comédie Française.

IV

JEAN-PAUL went into the Carmelite chapel. The eight o'clock Mass was just over, and those who had taken Communion had stayed on, bowed deep in prayer. He knew that Marthe came often to this Mass, but would not admit to himself that he had come there in the hope of seeing her.

At first, not catching sight of her, he felt sad, and, kneeling down, hid his face in his hands. 'Thou knowest, O God,' he murmured, 'that I am not in love with her . . . that I have never felt the wish to live with her always, that I feel no emotion when I touch her forehead with my lips.'

Just then, he saw her coming towards him. She looked grave and solemn, and her face was rather pale. There was a far-away expression in her eyes, as though she had not yet emerged from an ecstatic vision. He joined her at the door.

'I'm on my way to meet papa at the Luxembourg,' she told him: 'come with me.'

They went into the gardens, where the leaves were already out on the trees. The air was filled with the cries of children and the twittering of birds. Hoops kept getting between their legs. They neither of them spoke, she still solemn, he feeling rather removed, and wondering why. He looked at her again. She awoke no desire in him. The simple straw hat she was wearing cast a flickering shadow on her face. She bought her usual little roll from the usual old woman who talked to her for a few moments about her rheumatism.

'Hold my prayer-book,' she said to Jean-Paul, and then

began slowly to nibble her roll. 'Why are you looking at me?'

'I don't know. . . . I like that simple dress. . . . I like the look in your eyes; it's as though you "weren't here" at all—the look of a young girl who goes to early Mass and has a pale face when she's fasting. . . .'

'Beware! you're talking dangerously like a book, dear cousin!'

'You're right, Marthe: I've got printer's ink in my veins instead of blood!'

And to himself he said, in the lowest of low voices: 'Who will rescue me?'

Then he smiled, aware that he was making himself ridiculous by indulging in such outmoded romanticism. A line by Jammes came to his lips:

Le jeune homme des temps anciens que je suis.

'There's papa!' exclaimed Marthe.

Monsieur Jules Balzon was coming towards them, dragging his feet, and looking diminutive in the heavy cape which he kept carefully buttoned in spite of the warmth of this early Spring day. He smiled at the two young people, and his blotchy face broke into a thousand wrinkles.

'Are you coming home with me, my dears?'

'Don't you want to take a walk, father?'

'No, I've got some exercises to correct. D'you know, Jean-Paul, there's one of my pupils who thinks it fun to quote Barrès in all his essays, no matter what the subject. He's fifteen! Very humiliating for me who never have understood what the fellow is after!'

'Dear uncle, you're making fun of me!'

'Not a bit of it. I've read Le jardin de Bérénice. The author explains what he means, in the Introduction, in several notes, and in a series of Prefaces, but I still don't understand. . . .'

Jean-Paul was careful not to leap to the defence of his favourite author. His elderly cousin's taste had always been for works which held a facile echo of Renan. It mattered little to him that their substance was mediocre. Anatole France was his ideal. It often irritated Jean-Paul to hear him holding forth in the manner of the intolerable Bergeret.

To change the subject, the young man started to question Monsieur Balzon about Lucile de Chateaubriand. For years, the Professor had been working with loving care on a book which he hoped would bring that sad young woman to life.

But Marthe, whose mind was elsewhere, said suddenly:

'Jean-Paul, are you going to Madame des Onges' tea to-morrow?'

He caught in the low and rather muffled voice an anxious note which tickled him.

'I don't know: those parties of hers always bore me to death.'

She was insistent:

'Oh, but you must, Jean-Paul! Yesterday, at the Burand-Martins, I was introduced to a very odd and unkempt young man. His mother, it seems, is dragging him round all the drawing-rooms. He knew you at school. . . . I think his name is Vincent Hiéron. . . . Here's a chance for you to renew an old friendship. . . . Do you remember him?'

'Oh yes, I remember him . . .' Jean-Paul said in a low voice.

The idea of seeing Vincent again, set his heart racing.

Hiéron was the friend to whom, under the school trees, he had confided his youthful melancholy. He could see again in memory the hollow cheeks, the eyes ablaze with passion. How fiery a spirit had dwelt in that frail body! Later, however,

Vincent had seemed to be avoiding him, infuriated by his dilettante attitude. Not to believe would have killed him, so frantic was his need to affirm.

Jean-Paul knew that Vincent was devoting himself entirely to an experiment in active Christian-Democracy, though what exactly this was he was not sure. He had, however, noticed, in the porch of Saint-François-Xavier, on Sundays, a number of pale and gentle individuals with flowing black ties. To what social class they belonged it was difficult to determine. They were engaged in selling a weekly magazine called *Amour et Foi*.

'He wants to see me again!' thought Jean-Paul, and suddenly felt within himself an upsurge of happiness such as he had not experienced since he was twenty.

He stopped in front of the old house in the rue Garancière in which the Balzons lived.

'My boy,' said the Professor, 'don't forget that we are counting on you for the Easter holidays.'

Just as he was taking his leave of them, the girl repeated her father's words:

'We are counting on you.'

Jean-Paul crossed the Place Saint-Sulpice where the boys and girls of the Catechism class were playing. A pauper's hearse was standing by the curb. Several of the boys were laughing and pushing round a newspaper kiosk. He thought of the Castelnau estate which lay out on the heath, only a mile distant from his father's house. It had been familiar to him in the years of his over-sensitive boyhood. In those days Marthe would hide behind the trees, thinking it fun to frighten him by jumping out suddenly, and then passionately kiss his tears away.

He saw again the unobtrusive country house, with its tremendously solid walls, which was always so cool in the oppressive summer heat. He remembered the apple-loft and its delicious smell of quince and old cupboards where, every afternoon, he and Marthe had had their tea, and he had wiped jammy fingers on his smock; the great drawing-room the ceiling of which was supported on a massive transverse beam; the clock with its figure of Ceres; the little Second-Empire 'poufs' covered in black silk studded with yellow buttons; the photograph album from the pages of which unknown ladies and gentlemen smiled out at him; the tall oil-lamps. . . . The park, too, he remembered, the grassy rides where, as children, they would stand 'listening to the silence' as Marthe used to say . . . or to the quiet monotonous moaning of the wind in the swaying pine-tops.

'O! childhood!' said Jean-Paul to himself: 'it is always to you that I find myself returning, you that I long to recover in a rambling old house. There were rooms in it which were never opened, and, on the mantelpieces, seashells brought back from distant voyages by persons now long dead. I remember how Marthe used to press them to my ear, and say, "listen to the sound of the sea!" '

The lift stopped at his landing.

He worked until the moment when, standing at the open window in the warm dusk, he could watch the daylight die, and feel his memories awaken. He thought: 'What happiness has the day brought me?' Then he smiled at the prospect of meeting Vincent Hiéron on the morrow, and saw again, in recollection, the schoolyard in the days when his friend already had a pale, tormented face, and was punished for not joining in the games of the other boys.

V

ENTLEMEN in frock-coats, gloomy but resigned, encumbered the passages, and were being begged in vain by their hostess to sit down. They remained heroically standing while, in the little clearing established in front of the fireplace, poet followed poet. Some were very old, but these, in spite of mottled cheeks and comic paunches, passionately declaimed the poetry of love. They awoke in Jean-Paul a faint sense of pity. . . . But the younger ones, with their defiant airs and bitter expressions, exasperated him; those in particular who had long hair and stock ties, and personally inscribed their names in the reporters' notebooks. . . . The whole literary performance produced an impression of poverty and mediocrity of which all those present appeared to be conscious. No sooner had the reader, with much shaking of hands and smiling acknowledgement of his colleagues' 'bravos', regained his seat, swollen to bursting with ineffable self-satisfaction, than a terrible silence fell upon the room. . . . Such talking as there was was conducted in low voices. Even the least intelligent seemed to be conscious of a sense of discomfort, though why, they could not explain. The ironists, surrounded by the poets, or by the friends and relations of the poets, did not know what to do with their irony. The violent were consumed by frustrated indignation, and the dilettanti, for whom the foolishness of mankind constitutes, as a rule, a pleasing spectacle, appeared to be overwhelmed by so excessive a display of the ridiculous.

Jean-Paul tried in vain to pick out Vincent Hiéron in the crowd. At last, worn-out and depressed, he sought refuge in the smaller drawing-room to which the noisy exhibitionism of the performers could not penetrate.

A single lamp diffused an air of peace. Here, he felt, the owners of the house must spend their leisure moments. The armchairs were, obviously, in constant use. A work-box depended from the lamp-stand . . . and, though Jean-Paul felt a certain degree of embarrassment at the thought of having broken in upon so intimate a place, he responded readily to the evidence of tranquillity and quiet thought. Silently he begged the pardon of all the objects to which he was a stranger, though they had so kindly an air, and sat down. The shutters had not been closed in front of the French windows, and he could see a tree in the garden outlined against a patch of still pale sky.

Two people came into the room. Jean-Paul, who was short-sighted, merely guessed that one of them was Marthe. He could see no more than her general shape, her bright, tawny hair, her pretence of a bosom . . . and, as always, found her anything but desirable. She turned to him. 'Is that you, Jean-Paul?'—she asked, and, turning to the young man at her side, added: 'Must I introduce you to your old friend?'

Her companion moved into the circle of light cast by the lamp. Jean-Paul murmured the name of his former school-fellow:

'Vincent. . . .'

How little he had changed! Jean-Paul recognized, as something long familiar, the look of proud suffering in the face, the frail body consumed, as it were, by a violent, unslaked spirit. . . . He called to mind the impatient claims made upon him by the boy in the long-ago, and could feel again the hissing lash of his contempt. Only the eyes gave evidence of a greater calm. In them was visible the peace of those who live in the constant presence of their God.

'Is it really you?'—he said.

'I recognized you as soon as I entered the drawing-room, Jean-Paul. Let me explain that I am in this crowd of fools only in obedience to my mother's wish. But, in a month's time I shall be twenty-one, and free to go where I wish!'

'But, since you recognized me, Vincent, why did you not make yourself known?'

As he spoke these words, Jean-Paul looked at Marthe. She understood the meaning of his glance and moved away—conscious that she meant but little to her beloved when a friend, or mere acquaintance, was with him.

'On the contrary,' replied Vincent: 'I hid myself the better to observe you.'

He studied the other closely for a moment, and then went on:

'Yes, you are still the same. . . . I had only to watch you moving from group to group in the drawing-room, just as you used to do in the playground, to know that . . . only to take note of your hesitation and your solitude, and of the way in which, each time somebody read his trivial ineptitudes, the corners of your mouth drooped. . . .'

They walked home together. Jean-Paul kept up a flow of talk, yielding to the desire he felt to unbosom himself to the friend he had just found again. He spoke of his incurable melancholy, of his weak will, of how mediocre life seemed to him.

'You used to say just the same things when we were at school, Jean-Paul, and you'll go on saying them until the day when you will have learned the meaning of *renunciation*.'

'That I cannot do. . . . I no longer belong to myself. . . . I seem to remember that, even in those days, you thought me "bookish".'

'The love of books, when all's said, Jean-Paul, is just love of oneself. One reads only those authors in whom one sees oneself reflected. But in worshipping himself, a man worships a very petty god. He fails to live because he is his own prisoner. Before any of us can truly live, he must renounce self. . . .'

He had something of that preacher's manner which young men assume who worry their heads over social and religious problems.

'I cannot . . . I cannot. . . .'

'I have prayed for you, Jean-Paul, even when you believed that I was far away. . . . I shall continue to pray until such time as you are freed from yourself . . . until such time as you have given yourself to God, and to God in your fellow-men.'

This spate of eloquence brought no smile to Jean-Paul's lips, for even at school he had heard the same voice saying the same things. He longed to be alone and free to weep.

They stopped talking, being constantly separated by the base familiars of the Boulevard Saint-Michel. Ah! how Jean-Paul detested those washed-out student faces, so many of them covered with pimples and gaping with meaningless laughter.

The two young men stopped in front of the house in the rue des Écoles in which Vincent was living.

'Have you heard of the *Amour et Foi* movement, *Love and Faith*, Jean-Paul?'—Vincent asked suddenly.

'I know it by name. I've often seen its red posters. . . . On one occasion I even attended a lecture by Jérome Servet. He runs the movement, doesn't he?'

'Quite correct. We must have a talk about it some time.'

They arranged to meet on the following day.

The children were leaving the Luxembourg Gardens. Only a few pairs of lovers still loitered there. Jean-Paul remained alone in the dwindling light. What a great gulf there was between his friend's mind and his own!

'He has returned to me only to save me'—he said to himself: 'what do I care about his saving me if he can't love me? . . . Besides, my heart is weary of all these conversions with relapse following inevitably on their heels. Always, after a religious crisis, I used to have the feeling that, in those passionate duologues between my soul and God, re-read in a mood of disgust, it was always I who made the running. Both the questions and the answers came from me. But my poor voice is not strong enough to play two parts for long.'

He remembered how he had always surrendered, unconditionally to the friend who had remained, almost invariably, silent. . . .

'How he stared at me!'—he thought.

Just then a monstrous motor-bus filled the rue des Saints-Pères with the rattle of old iron. He shut his eyes.

VI

VINCENT HIÉRON, lost in thought, was making his way down the rue Barbet-de-Jouy. Well-fed menservants with solemn expressions were busy polishing brass door bells. Two ladies, dressed in black, with heavy prayer-books in their hands, and the lingering traces of joy and mystic ecstasy on their white, smooth faces, smiled, thinking, no doubt of the chocolate and toast which they would soon be enjoying—always with a keener appetite on the morning when they had taken Communion. . . . A deep, low-hung *coupé* was waiting in front of a carriage entrance, and the young footman, his eyes still puffy with sleep, his lips shining from a lavish breakfast, turned a scornful eye on Vincent of whose shabby overcoat and flowing tie he doubtless disapproved.

Vincent was quite insensitive to this atmosphere of tranquil, catholic and exclusive luxury. In the rue de Babylone he entered the front entrance of a modern building, overloaded with those ornamental motifs which were so much in favour with the building contractors of the day. On the first-floor balcony the words *Amour et Foi* were displayed in enormous letters. Several young men, with the air of busy ants, were going in and out. Vincent Hiéron crossed a lobby the walls of which were covered with red posters and proclamations. Some of the youths shook hands with him as he passed. Some of them addressed him by his christian name, putting into that

'Vincent' a warm tenderness expressive both of familiarity and respect.

He replied with a brief gesture of salutation, and went upstairs. On the first landing he pushed aside a curtain behind which was a door. The room to which it gave access was low and windowless. A bronze fist, which seemed to leap from the wall, held a sconce which diffused a glow of electric light. A mask of Pascal, hanging below an austere Jansenist Christ, showed vivid against a silk hanging with the colour of dead leaves. Vincent passed behind a second curtain and found himself in the office where Jérome was waiting for him. He was standing with his face pressed to the window, his clenched fists deep in the pockets of a stained and shapeless jacket. Those who loved him never noticed the badly knotted tie, the untidy hair, the common mouth in a heavy face, the massive neck, the pendulous, unshaven cheeks. All they saw were the wonderful eyes, deep-set eyes which could see far into the hearts of men, the beautiful, delicate, long-fingered hands which habitually reached out to grasp the hands of those he wished to conquer, closing on them, holding them with imperious authority. . . . He turned round with a smile.

'You've turned up, dear Vincent, just when I was feeling sad, and most wanted you with me.'

Vincent flushed with pleasure. He was one of those who felt a thrill whenever he heard that voice, and, with the thrill, a sense of joy renewed.

'Sure I'm not in the way? that you're not working?'

'No, dear boy, I'm feeling tired. . . . If you only knew. . . .'

He sat down at his desk, his arms hanging loose. . . .

'Bad news from Rome? . . .'

'Rather . . . one of those equivocal letters which only *they* know how to write, all guarded praise, reticence, and threats

couched in benedictory phrases. But I know that Monsignor
Bonaud, who forbids his seminarists and his priests to attend
our meetings or to read our magazine, has the support of the
Vatican. His example will be followed. I have had despairing
letters from many of the seminary pupils. . . .'

'That is the measure of your success, Jérome. The bishop
may impose on them a formal discipline, but what does that
matter if their hearts and minds escape him and remain in
passionate subjection to you?'

Jérome smiled again. 'That's a terrible thing to say, dear
Vincent.'

'Ah! Jérome, let us forget politics and all these odious tricks.
The life of ardour and enthusiasm which once was ours, when
the world knew nothing of us, was so fine, so wonderful! Do
you remember how we used to go into the industrial slums . . .
where in the back room of some wineshop you used to
address the men we found there? At first your words were
interrupted by gross mocking and coarse laughter. But, little
by little, those poor souls were pricked into wakefulness.
Faces took on a look of gravity till then quite strange to them,
and you, seeing the change, could speak at last to them of
Christ.'

'Yes, indeed, I do remember. . . .'

'Ah! Jérome, those walks home through the winter nights,
with the rain on our faces, or in the warm Spring darkness, our
eyes turned to the sky with its load of stars between the serried
roof-tops. . . .'

'I have not forgotten, Vincent.'

'And then, Montmartre . . . Montmartre. Do you remember
how we used to climb of an evening, in silence, to the great
basilica? Women and men passed us, singing choruses. The
windows of the cabarets were aglow with light. The illu-

minated sails of the Moulin Rouge turned and turned above a vile and sinful world. . . . We would enter the basilica, and then began our long, exhausting but delicious vigil. From time to time we would go into the Sacristy to snatch a few moments rest. You read to us the *Mystère de Jésus*. . . . How profoundly we believed in our cause in those days! How bright the spirit burned in us! I really held the faith, then, that we were going to give France back to Jesus Christ. . . .'

Jérome made a gesture of protest.

'But nothing has changed since then, nothing!'

'Everything has changed, Jérome. We are now a Power in the land. We have papers of our own. We have a political programme. Our spiritual superiors suspect us. Our former sympathizers are deserting us. . . .'

'Betraying is the truer word. . . .'

'They no longer understand us. We do not now speak the same language to them.'

Vincent broke off, appalled by his own daring.

'That's enough, boy, that's enough!'—cried the Master in curt, imperious tones. 'I shall begin to think that you are tempted to be one of them.'

'I abandon you, Jérome? How can you believe such a thing? Don't you know that I am yours for ever?'

The Master took his two hands, and looked fixedly at him.

'Yes, I know that you are one of the faithful, that I can rely on you. . . .'

Abruptly he changed the subject. 'What about this Jean-Paul Johanet, this friend of yours whom we might use on the paper: have you seen him again?'

'Yes, he will be an easy conquest. He swims in a tide of books, and spends long afternoons alone, analysing his empty, complicated little mind.'

C

'It is precisely at that stage that one must lay hold on men's minds'—said Jérome: 'when they have no resistance left, when they can be seized and held.'

'You must be careful how you go,' said Vincent: 'Jean-Paul is not wholly without character. He will certainly put up a show of resistance.'

The Master showed signs of suspicion. 'That'll be too bad: what I want round me are temperaments ready to serve my ends, not characters trying to resist me. . . . So long, my boy. If you see anyone waiting at my door, say that I am seeing nobody.'

Vincent took his leave. A very young man was waiting under the mask of Pascal.

'Jérome is tired and can see nobody,' said Vincent, very gently.

A look of pain showed in the other's haggard eyes. For a few days he had tasted the pleasure of being the beloved disciple. With a set expression he stood aside to let Vincent pass. He did not even greet him.

'Poor lad'—thought Vincent, as he went down the stairs. 'Why should he resent me? Won't just the same thing happen to me one of these days? . . . But there is someone greater than this man, someone for whom I have made far fewer sacrifices, yet He will love me eternally. . . .'

Meanwhile, no sooner was Jérome left alone than he lowered the blind, kneeled down on the carpet, and, covering his face with his hands, began to pray. The memories evoked by Vincent came back into his mind. It seemed all so long ago, and he was frightened. In those days he had set out with a handful of young men to seek the Kingdom of God, and to establish justice among men. . . .

Now, from all sides, he was being attacked. It was from

Christians sharing the same baptism as himself, professing the same faith, that the worst abuse, the grossest calumnies, were coming. His fellow-men had forsaken him, and he was now alone with his ideal, surrounded only by over-emotional young people, whose adoration had sown in him the seed of pride. . . .

And so, he kneeled and prayed. Since leaving school, Jérome had broken free from all the formulae of devotion. He spoke with God as a man might speak with his friend. But he had read too much, and often served up to his Heavenly Father, in the guise of prayer, remembered snippets from Ibsen or Tolstoy. Frequently, too, in the middle of a prayer, he would feel himself being swept away by a cry that mounted to his lips. This he would note down, and later use in the peroration of a lecture, when it would be uttered in a voice to which he had imparted a deliberate quiver, and would strike deep into the heart of some expectant listener.

'Is it true, Father, that I no longer seek your kingdom? Is it only for my own glory that I set so many young hearts dreaming, burning, suffering?'

The contempt with which he felt that he treated all honours bestowed by men, reassured him.

'As on that very first day, Lord'—he murmured—'your presence within me fills me with a love sufficient to transform the world and found in it the Kingdom of Justice, that your will may be done *on earth* as it is in Heaven.

'It is your good news that I long to spread among the numberless persons on whom You once had mercy, but whom the wicked have convinced that your Gospel and your Church condemn the hopes they have of a more just, a more fraternal City. . . .

'Is it true that I am working only for myself? You know,

Father, that I have desired nothing in this world but love. For a long time now, however, I have become resigned to being of the number of those whom You have exiled from the love of their fellow-men. These poor little ones who do love me are, in my eyes, nothing more than so many souls to be thrown into the flowing waters which lead to You.'

He rose to his feet and looked long at the photographs which covered the walls, recognizing many of the eyes that looked out from them, many of the smiles. One young man, he remembered, had walked with him at night on a road bathed in moonlight after a lecture he had given in some small town the name of which he had forgotten. They had been returning slowly, on foot, to the country house in which a room had been prepared for him. The young man in question —who had spent a lonely boyhood in a small sub-Prefecture— had trembled with joy at finding himself in the presence of the great spirit who had come all that distance to bring to him the word of life. Jérome remembered the lecture—a battle from which he had emerged as victor, in which he had silenced a noisy, hostile crowd. . . . But why did he remember the walk back through the sleeping countryside? A supernatural light had given the appearance of infinity to the great stretches of ploughed land. A farmstead with a barking dog had lain slumbering almost on a level with the ground, its garden and its outbuildings huddled round it. . . .

Jérome let his thoughts dwell on that young unknown whom the wonderful walk under the stars had raised far above his normal self. His presence at that time had been sufficient to fill the Master's heart. . . . What could one not find, at certain times, in the eyes of even the humblest of human beings? That stupid, dreary creature had, for once in his life, achieved sublimity when Jérome spoke to him.

Many of the others had written on their photographs—
*To Jérome—my only friend: For him who revealed the Truth to
me:*—poor little faces whose smiles awakened no memory in
his heart!

Jérome Servet felt within himself that exaltation from which
great works may emerge. He rang the bell. His secretary came
in. He began to dictate.

VII

IN the alleys of the Luxembourg Gardens the nurses were collecting spades and buckets and skipping-ropes preparatory to departure. Round the artificial water, and on the terraces, little boys and girls were still chasing one another with birdlike cries.

Jean-Paul walked quietly, seeking the unfrequented paths. He was building up for himself the ideal of a grave and serious life which should be filled with religion and the consideration of social problems. A silent tune accompanied his dreaming, but, though it sounded only in his heart, he could hear it plainly, as though diffused in the surrounding air. It was the song which Verlaine, turned sober, had once written:

> Elle dit, la voix reconnue,
> Que la bonté c'est notre vie,
> Que de la haine et de l'envie
> Rien ne reste, la mort venue. . . .

He quickened his step. . . . The moment was close at hand when Vincent would come, as he came every evening, to speak to him about the Cause. In listening to his friend's brusque threats and entreaties, Jean-Paul found a curious and delicious pleasure. Already a star of hope was rising and shining on his devastated heart—the hope that he might one day turn his back on pride, on disquiet, on all the complications of his life: that he would be fervent at early Mass on each day of the week: that he would take Communion with passionate abandonment in a crowd of humble women, and then make one of a group of other austere and pure-hearted young men, to share their lives of piety, grave friendships and unobtrusive mission-work. . . . Such were the wishes that Jean-Paul discovered in himself. . . .

Peace came to him and he breathed a prayer. He left the Gardens and, in the soft darkness of the oncoming night, went into Saint-Sulpice. The Lady Chapel was almost deserted. All it contained in the way of humanity were a few shadowy incarnations of grief, poverty and humble wretchedness, upon their knees in prayer. In thought he made his pain one with their pain, though he knew not what it was. He said:

'O God! Thou who hast given me grace to understand Thy hours of darkness, and to weep before their mystery, Thou knowest with what dreams I have peopled them. It was Thy pleasure, nonetheless, never to trouble the current of my life. Thou hast made for me a calm existence in a peaceful room with the companionship of books. My Lord and my God, what can I say in my defence? . . . This only can I find to say, that much shall be forgiven me because I have not loved much. Between Thy justice and me flow all the tears of my youth.

'In the worst of my wanderings something in me has always cried to Thee. O my God! may those hours be counted unto me for righteousness when I loved Thee in the dim light of chapels! . . .'

In the street, among the moving crowds of those who, for all their weariness, found happiness in the prospect of the night to come when men can sleep and love, Jean-Paul's mood became less exalted. He thought of the Congress of *Amour et Foi* which was to be held in Bordeaux. He could spend a few weeks in that city before going on to pass the rest of his holidays at Johanet. Speaking to himself, he murmured:

'I know that Jérome Servet is a skilled Hunter of Souls. . . . May he take mine, with all its load of weariness and disgust: may he lift the burden from me and fill me with enthusiasm and love for an unknown Ideal. . . . How happily would I sacrifice the freedom which, till now, has brought me nothing but tears!

'Is it not better to become the slave of God, of a Master, of a doctrine, than to remain young and free, but solitary and tired, and, now and then wishing for death? . . . Vincent has told me that in the *Amour et Foi* Movement I shall find good and humble brethren, who will teach me how to share the hopes by which they live. . . .'

Thus, in docile mood, did the young man bend his head to receive the yoke. But the nature of the Ideal towards which he was moving, was still unknown to him. He advanced, as it were, backwards, his eyes fastened on ancient horrors, his stomach retching with the bile of daily living. He was hastening to what might be, perhaps, the Truth, though his only purpose was to free himself from those gloomy fits of melancholy which were driving him to his death.

VIII

A FEW hours later he was dressing for a ball. Vincent, seated in an armchair, was begging him to put in an appearance at the Congress organized by *Amour et Foi*. But Jean-Paul who had quite made up his mind to let himself be convinced, found it rather fun to start by saying no.

'I have so little faith, Vincent, and of love, nothing at all. I believe in scarcely anything but the vanity of all effort, and of what you call social action. . . .'

Vincent got irritably to his feet. 'We are not just isolated units, my poor friend. Even the humblest of our acts is not without its effect upon the whole. . . .'

'But even the most important have repercussions only on those who are very close to us'—Jean-Paul replied. 'Even God —if it be a fact that He made Himself man—could reveal His truth only to a few million souls. The immense crowd of human beings never had knowledge of Him.'

'He is revealed in the hearts of all of us: no man can escape that inner revelation.'

'If we continue this argument much longer, I shan't arrive at the Onges' until the cotillion is due to start.'

'Get along then, but I'm counting on seeing you next Sunday at the public session. . . . Since you've got to pass through Bordeaux on your way to Johanet, it's merely a question of starting three weeks earlier than you would have done.'

'What about my work?'

'Take your books with you.'

'I'll think about it.'

Left to himself, Jean-Paul concentrated on the task of dressing. The room was brightly lit. At the foot of the bed his pumps showed two spots of light. His evening shirt with its starched front, lay gleaming on an armchair.

In the cab, Jean-Paul, embarrassed by his white gloves, realized that he had not got the fare ready. He fumbled in his purse under the suspicious gaze of the driver. A fifty-centime piece—perhaps a ten-franc one—rolled in the gutter.

Leaning with his back to a door, he watched the little tulle clouds revolving, and on top of each, a solemn, stupid little face with the same fixed smile as all the other faces had.

'Why aren't you dancing, Jean-Paul?'

Marthe was there before him, slim and smiling. She was wearing a pastel-blue dress which clung closely to her body and was so narrow at the bottom that it was a wonder she could dance at all. To Jean-Paul she looked like a very delicately made girl in her nightgown. But while they exchanged quite meaningless phrases he was thinking that he had only to raise a finger to have legitimate possession, in a large double bed, of the body at which he could guess beneath the filmy stuff. They chatted. A scrap of lace showed in the low-cut opening of her bodice. But what charmed Jean-Paul was the delicious curve made by her hair behind her ears.

'Marthe, I'm going to leave you. . . .'

'You're going?'

Colour came flooding to her cheeks.

'I'm going to Bordeaux with Vincent. Later, in a month's time, I shall come on to you in the country.'

'Monsieur Hiéron, I can see, is practising his good works on you,' said Marthe in a more cheerful voice.

He protested.

'I don't yet belong to *Amour et Foi*. . . .'

'Oh, *amour et toi*!'—she smiled, though not very convincingly.

'What exactly do you mean, Marthe?'—he asked, with a look of irritation on his face.

Suddenly Marthe's pale eyes clouded over. She stared at the chandelier in an effort to keep from crying. She moved a bunch of roses from side to side in front of her face. At the sight of this gentle little creature who loved him, Jean-Paul was momentarily caught up on a wave of sadness. But, just at that moment a Boston struck up, and, putting an arm round her waist, he started to revolve with her, without a single thought in his head.

IX

A WEEK later, in his bedroom at the Hôtel de France in Bordeaux, Jean-Paul stood at the window, going over in his mind the hours of delicious agitation through which he had been recently living. He had let himself be carried away by the unbridled emotion of the public meetings. He had joined in the shouting, and trembled when the savage words of the *Internationale*, like a storm of wind, had bowed the timid heads and swept aside the facile clerical commonplaces. He had felt like crying when Jérome Servet had flung at a crowd, silent at last and dominated, the words— Mercy, Love. . . .

He had abandoned himself to the pleasure of knowing himself to be an unthinking unit in an assembly of young men worked to a high pitch of fanaticism, while Jérome spoke of the mysterious strength which the faithful could find in the Eucharist, a strength which made possible every extreme of heroism and martyrdom. . . .

But what he chiefly remembered was the private meeting at which, one evening at six o'clock, Jérome, in a voice hoarse with exhaustion and emotion, had addressed them.

It had been held in one of the class-rooms of the State school. The dusk filtered through the windows with the song of birds. Jérome had said—what had he said? Jean-Paul no longer knew. An extraordinary emotion had overwhelmed him. He had been dazzled by the light of Truth unveiled: 'Joy . . . joy . . . tears of joy. . . .' He remembered that he had wept silently in

42

a corner of the room, and that Jérome had quoted the words used by Pascal in his *Mystère de Jésus*:

'Jesus will endure His agony in the garden until the end of the world . . . during all that time we must not sleep. . . .' He recalled how he had trembled when Jérome had begged them to extend the bounds of their own poor lives, to make them infinite by giving them to an infinite Cause. . . .

Then, the comrades had gone away one by one. Only Jérome, Vincent and Jean-Paul were left in the little playground where the light was fading, and the single plane tree was noisy with the twittering of birds. . . .

Jérome had laid his hands upon the young man's shoulders, had looked into his eyes with infinite sweetness and power, and had asked in a voice that trembled:

'Are you ready to give everything to the Cause . . . everything?'

Then had Jean-Paul uttered from his heart, the last cry of the *Mystère de Jésus*: 'To Thee, O God, I give everything!'

Then Jérome had taken him in his arms, and said:

'You have given yourself, Jean-Paul: you are no longer your own property. Live from now on for the souls of men.'

To live for the souls of men—that was the new life he was being offered, that was the road he must follow, which showed so plain on a Summer's morning when pilgrims moved along it, singing. . . . To live for men's souls, to give himself to those souls!—He spoke again the liberating words. . . .

'I am delivered,' he thought: 'this is truly *my night*.' All the will-power he had believed was dead fermented in him: his heart was, at one and the same time, at peace and passionate, as it had been on the evening of the day when he had made his First Communion.

There was a knock at the door. Jean-Paul saw with dismay

Monsieur Balzon and Marthe come into the room, dressed for travelling.

'I am given to understand that you did not, after all, reserve rooms for us. . . .'

Jean-Paul looked at the old gentleman's round eyes, at his shining pate spotted with innumerable drops of sweat. . . .

He had forgotten. He had got into the way recently of forgetting all commissions . . . but of this one he had been reminded at least twenty times. . . . Monsieur Balzon, who hated the uncertainties and surprises of life, made no bones about expressing his annoyance:

'The hotel is full, and we are not leaving for the country until the day after tomorrow. . . . There is a name, Jean-Paul, for this kind of thoughtlessness . . . egotism, pure and simple. . . .'

The old gentleman went off in search of his luggage and of two vacant rooms. His shrill voice could be heard echoing through the corridors.

'I have other things to worry me,' said Jean-Paul to Marthe, when they were alone. 'I have just lived through two days of enthusiasm and joy. . . .'

Marthe gave unqualified approval to the new part he was playing, the 'man of action'.

'You must let me have your impressions at Castelnau, when you come, two days from now.'

'That will be out of the question, Marthe. I shan't be seeing you for three weeks. I have to stay on in Bordeaux with Vincent Hiéron. He and I are going to organize an *Amour et Foi* group here.'

'Oh dear, how disappointing . . . how disappointing. . . .' The young girl could only repeat the words mechanically.

But at this moment, looking fresh, and smiling, Monsieur

Balzon returned. He had managed to find two rooms, and had had their luggage moved into them. . . . He had come back now to explain what had happened. . . . His vexation had been little more than a matter of form. In his heart of hearts he was delighted at the prospect of having his daughter to himself.

'You're not likely to be bored, Jean-Paul. I once spent ten years in Bordeaux and I can assure you that it is a delightful city. Its principal curiosity is the great wine magnates. Their calling confers, here, a sort of patent of nobility. They can be seen, each day, from five to seven, in the Cours de l'Intendance and the Allées de Tourny, looking at one another out of the corners of their eyes, and pretending all the time that they are entirely unaware of the proximity of their competitors. . . .'

Before undressing, Marthe sat for a while at the window, leaning her elbow on the sill, and her cheek on her hand. The sounds of an orchestra came from a nearby Café. The night was warm, and so clear that she could see the masts and yards of ships showing black at the far end of the rue Esprit-des-Lois. . . . How inaccessible, she thought, was the heart of her beloved. . . . She had so much hoped to get a little closer to him during these holidays . . . but now she must give up the idea. She dreamed, but her dream was all of humility. All she wanted was to devote herself utterly, to make a total gift of everything she was and had, wishing for no reward other than that of going on giving, of living to serve him. . . . She did not ask to be loved—that would be too great a happiness, a happiness so excessive that she thought it would kill her. . . .

She was on the verge of tears. There was a tightness in her throat . . . and, suddenly, tears and sobs broke from her like a storm of rain.

X

THE room was small and brightly lit. A whispering and inattentive audience of young men was listening to Jean-Paul's lecture—they were like schoolboys who attach no value whatever to what the master has to say. Two or three of them bore the marks of careful upbringing in one or other of the religious schools, but most of them were neatly dressed apprentices, whose calloused hands and black nails alone showed that they were not, say, students in Law School. There was a barber's assistant, his hair shining with the scrapings of his employer's pomade pots, and a number of respectable working-men who had reached *Amour et Foi* by way of workers' clubs.

'Just as slavery was replaced by bond-service which, in its turn, gave way to the modern wage-earning system . . . so, my friends, it would be wrong to think of the employer-employed pattern as being eternal. . . .'

Almost without realizing that he was doing so, Jean-Paul reeled off all the old stock-in-trade commonplaces of democratic theory. His eyes wandered idly over the ranks of his bored listeners.

His attention was suddenly drawn by two brown, attentive eyes set in a drab face to which a sagging mouth and a prematurely lined forehead gave an air of melancholy. The body, in its dark-red knitted pullover was muscular, and the large, chapped hands seemed unable to adapt themselves to an idleness which was strange to them. . . .

In the hope of giving a little more life to the proceedings, Jean-Paul fired off an ancient gibe at the expense of the bourgeoisie, which he happened to remember on the spur of the moment, and at once the young workman's mouth widened in a grin, a very youthful grin, which revealed a set of decayed teeth. . . . Jean-Paul had the gratifying impression that at least one person was paying attention to what he said. A note of restrained passion came into his voice, and he saw the brown eyes sparkle. It was as though from somewhere very far away a light flashed for a moment between the sickly lids.

Then, quoting stirring words from the writings of Lacordaire and Montalembert, he spoke about the pure delights of friendship, and announced that no longer was there any barrier between apprentices and students. He painted a picture of a society in which diverse minds and temperaments could be brought together within the limits of a shared faith. No doubt he was genuinely convinced for the time being of the truth of what he was saying. From then on, his listeners gave signs of being passionately interested.

'We may have our moments of doubt, dear comrades, but in them we shall be comforted by the sense of a friend's heart, a friend's soul close at hand to give us strength, and we shall enjoy that happiness which others know nothing of. . . .'

The speaker was no other than the Jean-Paul, the sensual, desiccated middle-class youth whom the least hint of vulgarity appalled, and the most excusable lack of elegance made physically sick. Many times during the past fortnight he had felt his head swim when he realized how wide was the gulf which separated him from his comrades, even from those of the same social standing as himself, who loved the People for reasons that did not come from books. Often, in the evening, after an exasperating period spent at a study-circle, he had taken refuge

D

in his room, conscious of an irresistible desire to get away from the working-class atmosphere of his surroundings! At such times he would put on a pair of delicately tinted pyjamas, and give an edge to his disgust by reading the taut verses of Jules Laforgue. . . .

At the back of the room the young workman was all ears. He seemed to feel that the lecturer's eloquence was directed at him alone.

And, indeed, it was to him that Jean-Paul picked his way when the lecture was over. The young man's name was Georges Élie; his employment that of a carpenter. At the Young Men's Club which he attended, the abbé had spoken to him about the *Amour et Foi* Movement. He had gone to a lecture given by Jérome Servet. It had, he said, 'knocked him sideways.'

'He was terrific,' he said—'absolutely. . . .'

It was painfully evident how difficult Georges Élie found it to put together the few threadbare words of his habitual vocabulary.

Jean-Paul took in the drawn, tired look of the boy's face, the mingled appearance of physical strength and exhaustion to be seen in those who have been set to work too young. The sight of the restless, melancholy eyes filled him with a great pity. He forgot that compassion, with him, was a short-lived emotion, and started to talk to Élie in a low voice. He spoke of the 'Cause', of the great moral revolution which Jérome Servet wanted to bring about in the proletarian outlook.

He said that now they were friends, nothing could separate them, since they were one with each other in faith and love.

The boy listened. A fierce, but, at the same time, sweet emotion made him feel that he wanted to cry.

'Is all this business about being my friend real?'

'Yes,' said Jean-Paul.

If only he had known all the treasure of meaning which the other packed into that word 'friend'! If only he had realized that it embodied all the craving for affection felt by a young creature whom life had brutalized, all the hunger for tenderness which was always being driven in upon itself!

They talked as they went back together through the empty Bordeaux streets at ten o'clock that night.

The apprentice entrusted to him the whole sensitive and scrupulous spirit of one who should have been a seminarist. He explained how lonely he felt at the workshop, spoke of the coarse mockery of which he was the victim. . . . Jean-Paul listened to him in a rather absent-minded way, and smiled, now and again, at Élie's racy local accent.

At the door of the hotel they parted. Jean-Paul felt a tiny prick of fear when the other said with a sort of brooding passion:

'This is for keeps, ain't it—you and me for always, old chap?'

For a fleeting instant the young bourgeois was tempted to destroy the poor fellow's illusion. He saw him already as someone ugly and common—someone whom he would never genuinely love, whom he was not worthy to love, to whom he would be the cause of much suffering. But he remembered his apostolic mission. Jérome Servet had said that one must give oneself to the service of men's souls, no matter how obscure, how degraded those men might be.

Conscious of the lie, which seemed to him heroic, he answered:

'Yes, dear boy, it's for ever.'

XI

A T six o'clock, when the workshop shut down, Georges
Élie soon got into the habit of accompanying Jean-
Paul on his evening walks. At first he knocked timidly
at the young man's door, and said, earnestly:—'sure I'm not
being a nuisance?' But Jean-Paul put so much kindness, so
much simplicity into his questions about how the other had
spent his day, felt so much pleasure in dazzling the limited
little mind, that Élie came, more and more each day, to confide
in him. He convinced himself that these visits of his gave
pleasure, at the very moment when Jean-Paul began to feel
bored by him.

At first, to be sure, he found him amusing company. He
thought it fun, at the hour of the day when the crowds were
at their thickest in the Cours de l'Intendance and the Allées de
Tourny, to show himself in public with a young workman
in a cloth cap, whose hands were coarse and whose wrists
were red. In the clear dusk he walked with Élie through the
well-dressed sauntering groups, all seeming to be marking
time, so that he regretted the hurly-burly of Paris—idly
answering the other's questions, and finding amusement in the
effect which his own words produced.

But after the first few days he began to feel that people had
grown used to seeing them together, and to find that conversation with Georges Élie was becoming increasingly empty
and pointless. *Amour et Foi* was the only subject they had in
common, and, even so, the same comments recurred again

and again. Jean-Paul only genuinely enjoyed the sort of literary
discussion in which he could quote the poetry of Jammes and
the Comtesse de Noailles, or glowing passages from Barrès
and Chateaubriand. He had a taste for producing unexpected
similies which made his friends in Paris laugh, but were quite
beyond Georges' comprehension. And, since, the young
bourgeois excelled in the vivid portraiture of human absur-
dities, it was a real trial for him to have to confine his talk to
admiring remarks about the 'stars' of *Amour et Foi* when he
was with his working-class friend.

In vain did he try to find entertainment in the other's stories
about life at the workshop and in the Boys' Club. The young
fellow bored him as his friends, even the most intelligent of
them, had done during his military service when, herded
together in barracks, they had talked on the assumption that
everybody was bound to be interested in tales about the
Captain's kindliness, or the brutality of the section-sergeant. It
was in just such a way that Élie discoursed about the humble
denizens of his own restricted world.

XII

ALONE in his room, Jean-Paul was reading Ollé-Laprune's *Prix de la Vie*. It was boring him horribly, though he would not admit it. Through the open window he could see the June sky, of a pale and washed-out blue, criss-crossed by the darting flight of swifts. A country smell hung over the city, and the distant sound of a brass-band came to him on the breeze.

He was peculiarly sensitive to all this joy of the still-young summer. Two lines by Francis Jammes came into his mind:

> . . . Quand, aux dimanches soirs,
> La grand'ville éclatait de légères fanfares. . . .

He looked for the volume, but the books published by the *Mercure de France* no longer encumbered his table as in the old days. Their places had been taken by pamphlets in which scholarly clerics set out to prove that the activities of the Inquisition, and the Massacre of Saint-Bartholomew could not be laid to the charge of the Church.

For a month now he had been devoting all his time and all his gifts to *the Cause*. The youthful democrats were filled with admiration of his fluency, of his frigid manner—of everything, in fact, which betrayed a man of the prosperous middle-class, in spite of his blouse and his flowing tie. . . .

But now, in this limpid dusk, he felt the need to conjure up memories of his past. Nowadays, he kept a careful watch even on his dreams, so as to remain absolutely chaste—but, this evening, he was obsessed by the recollection of former delights, and was conscious of a desire to wake again the memory of self-indulgences which he could never forget.

Vincent Hiéron quietly opened the door. 'Aren't you coming to the meeting of the Comrades, Jean-Paul?'

The young man did not stir from his armchair.

'No,' he said: 'I'm feeling tired this evening. It's as though there were a crack in my soul through which enthusiasm is oozing drop by drop.'

'What a romantic you are, my poor Jean-Paul! . . . that mood will vanish with the dusk.'

'One thing there is that does not vanish, Vincent, the past, my past, by which, at the moment, I am obsessed.'

'You don't regret it, surely?'

'How can I be certain'—said Jean-Paul—'that I don't regret the afternoons I used to spend in libraries with my eyes glued to books I didn't read . . . the times of brooding by my fire in the failing light of late afternoon, when I hadn't enough will-power left even to light my lamp?'

'How ridiculous you were in those days, Jean-Paul. . . .'

'And my aimless walks through the indifferent streets when, to keep myself amused, I let my imagination create the most marvellous legends. I used to cast myself for the role of famous author or musical genius, or, alternatively, summoned up the face of some passionate and indulgent woman. I saw myself in fancy waiting for her on a park bench on a night in June. I would watch her walking towards me down a path with hastening steps—and the blurred vision of her face under a half-veil, the sudden brightness of her eyes as she caught sight of me, the clasp of her ungloved hand—flooded my heart with infinite delight. . . . Then the vision would fade. . . . I felt more painfully my actual solitude. I went home and wrote poetry. . . .'

'All very puerile and gloomy'—said Vincent: 'you used to read it to me sometimes. I can still remember bits'—and he murmured:

Je vois dans chaque nuit, celle du bien-aimé,
Celle qui mènera vers moi mon coeur étonné
L'ami pour qui s'amasse en moi comme un automne
D'amitiés mortes et d'amours abandonnés. . . .

For a moment or two Vincent and Jean-Paul sat silent, on the brink of the past. . . . Vincent passed a hand across his forehead.

'Such memories are morbid,' he said. 'Are you coming?—we're very late.'

'Not this evening: I'm tired.'

'I know what's the matter with you,' replied Vincent, who was rather strung up, and could not forgive himself for having shown emotion, for having recited Jean-Paul's verses:—'the *mal de siècle*, that's what you're suffering from, the *mal de René*! How long are you going to let yourself be choked by all that romantic lumber?'

'For so long,' said Jean-Paul dreamily, 'as the idealism of youth finds itself up against the brutality and mediocrity of life. . . .'

A chambermaid came in to say that a Monsieur Élie was asking for him.

'O! again!'—muttered Jean-Paul. 'Say I'm out.'

'But . . . I've already said you're in, sir.'

'Then ask him to come up'—broke in Vincent Hiéron. Then, turning to his friend:

'What's biting you? That's the way to get yourself thoroughly disliked!'

'I can't help it. The fellow's a crashing bore! I find him in the hall every morning now, when I go out, and in the evening, when I get back: and a letter comes from him each afternoon. He wants to talk to me about *the Cause*. He's smothering me under the weight of his friendship. . . .'

'You're mad, my poor Jean-Paul! Have you forgotten the unselfishness of Jérome and the student-comrades? Are you concerned only to find pleasure in the traffic of souls?'

'I'm afraid I'm beginning to think so. . . . Anyhow, that boy's getting on my nerves, and he knows it: but back he comes like a faithful dog one's thrown into the water. . . .'

Just then, Élie came into the room. He was carrying, with some show of embarrassment, an astonishing hat of battered, greenish felt. . . . He advanced apprehensively, shamefacedly, and there really was in his eyes the sentimental expression of a dog that knows it is being a nuisance. . . . Vincent Hiéron, who foresaw a storm, shook him by the hand, and made himself scarce.

'I'm busy this evening, old man, very busy . . .'—and without another word, Jean-Paul started to cut the pages of *La Porte Etroite* by André Gide, with careful deliberation.

'Then I'll clear out,' said Élie, who did not want to understand. 'When can I see you?'—he added in a choked voice.

The fact that he had not understood put Jean-Paul completely out of patience. Thinking that it was his duty to undeceive him, he murmured in a very low voice, words which seemed to be even more unkind:

'We see one another almost every evening at *Amour et Foi*. Have we got to meet at other times, too? I'm working, and I need all the time I can spare from *the Cause*. . . .'

Before he had finished speaking, Élie, with a furious gesture, put on the hat, and went out, slamming the door so violently that some photographs stuck in the frame of the looking-glass over the fireplace, fell to the floor.

It grew dark. Jean-Paul, leaning on the window-sill, looked at the sky streaked by a last flight of swallows. The clock of a nearby Convent struck the hour. Close at hand, a woman was shrieking abuse at a child. Jean-Paul felt the old familiar anguish flood into his heart, like one of those high-tides which, at fixed seasons, flow back up the beach.

XIII

FROM then on, the comrades avoided him. They referred to him only as the 'bourgeois' or the 'intellectual'. He had suddenly come to attach enormous importance to a good education. 'It can take the place of almost everything else'—he reflected. . . . One evening, in the *Amour et Foi* club-room, a working printer, who prided himself on being 'literary', made some heavily abusive references to *l'Étape*. Jean-Paul greeted his remarks with a smile, the bitter smile with which the comrades were already familiar. Often, when referring to some article, or lecture, by Jérome, his ironical comments had revealed to them what is meant by the 'critical approach'.

But at meetings of *Amour et Foi* it was extremely dangerous to indulge a sense of the ridiculous. This was made very clear to him.

'I notice as you're not applauding, *sir*,' said Georges Élie, very pointedly.

Jean-Paul's contempt had left an incurable wound in the young workman's over-sensitive heart. Hatred was now a living reality in that narrow mind which one only love could have filled for a lifetime. . . . It made the shy young product of the Boys' Club almost unrecognizable.

'There's some things as the bourgeois'll never cotton to'— he said loudly, after the lecture.

'I'm beginning to wonder why them bourgeois comes here

at all'—struck in the speaker who, intimidated by Jean-Paul had cut his lecture short.

Curious looks were directed at the young man. There was a touch of pallor on his face, of that selfsame pallor which used to make Marthe say, when they were children,—'*You're in a wax.*' He continued to smile well aware that by doing so he was deliberately exasperating the comrades.

'The bourgeois come to teach you,' he said in a tone of deceptive gentleness. 'In turning up here they are more meritorious than you are, because in order to do so they give up more attractive ways of spending an evening. . . .'

There was an outburst of violent protests. A lot of other young men had gathered round to listen to the discussion.

Jean-Paul was looking over their heads. Through the pipe-smoke, and among the violent red of the various posters, he could see a portrait of Leo XIII giving the papal blessing. He was conjuring up for himself a vision of the wide open spaces which lay beyond the constricting walls, of the clear, cold night and the untroubled solitude.

'You need teaching a lot more than what we do,' said Georges Élie. 'You've got everything to learn from us . . . you . . . you parasites. . . .'

'How you do cling to your class prejudices!' replied Jean-Paul bitterly.

Suddenly, and for the first time, he realized that the whole doctrine of this 'Movement' was no longer a living reality for him but a collection of shoddy formulae which he had accepted uncritically, which, unaided, could never have attracted him into the company of these young men. . . . To himself he said:

'I was seeking a private happiness.'

At this moment, Vincent Hiéron came in. He was feared

rather than loved. There was an embarrassing silence. Then, groups began to form. Jean-Paul hastily shook his friend's hand, and went out. He could feel his throat contracting as it used to do when he was a child and trying not to cry.

Shopkeepers and concierges were busily chatting on the doorsteps. Little girls were skipping. On the Place Pey-Berland he could see the glow of the Cathedral windows. . . . 'It's the last day of Mary's Month,' he told himself, and went in.

Among the lilies the illuminated Virgin stood, herself like a lily. Several poor women and goggling children were kneeling outside the Choir railings, and children's voices—the celestial timbre of which would soon be breaking—were singing those old canticles which are so heavily charged with ecstasy and ancient fervour. . . . In one of the side-chapels Jean-Paul at last succumbed to tears. They moistened his hands. They smelt as they had done when, at six years old, he used to cry in the silence of his room when his mother had failed to rock him to sleep upon her lap.

He went back to the hotel, and, stretched on a chaise-longue, set himself methodically to trace his sense of gloomy lassitude to its cause. . . . Throughout a quiet and lonely childhood he had got into the habit of watching himself live.

'Was not the enthusiasm I felt during the Congress'—he thought—'due, in the last analysis, to my belief that I had at last found a purpose in life? Was it not a flowering of my personality in which my tormenting pride found pleasure? At that time I was so terribly unhappy! My misery had nothing to do with the material circumstances of my exis-tence—except, perhaps, those digestive troubles which always incline one to melancholy. No; I was conscious of my own mediocrity. Even to-day I am painfully aware of all I am not, and often doubt the value of such small gifts as I may have. . . . Before ever I came across *Amour et Foi* I had got beyond enjoying even my own wretchedness, as once I did in the long dusks of my adolescence, when I found it reflected in the books I read. It is that same past, that sad and gloomy past, which has again caught up with me to-night. I am, in very truth, its prisoner. It clothes in the cadences of wordless poetry the poor pleasures of that long-vanished time. It brings the heavy memory of ancient faults. It is that past which has brought me to a halt upon the path of austerity, along which, only yesterday, I was moving so joyfully—too joyfully, alas! because even now I think that I might find some pleasure in mingling with the comrades. But is that the same as the joy of the disciple who has done a little good to the souls which he has met with on his way?

'To-night I realize that I am turning to my own account the mission work on which I have embarked, that, actually, I have found it all great fun.

'I was always an amateur of souls, and in *Amour et Foi* I found myself in a position to travel through lands of which, till then, I had known nothing. I leaned with pleasure above the standing waters on which I had happened by chance, and sometimes there came from them the sound of a tender and mysterious voice. This or that soul to whose interests I thought I was devoting all my efforts, did nothing more than add an item to my collection.

'Yet, how sincerely I believed that I loved, how genuinely, in fact, I did love, all you workers of the mournful countenance, with your sad, tormented faces—especially those of you who, wholly without education, came to listen to what I had to say. . . . Deeply etched within myself I carry the image of those colourless faces to which a tired and drooping mouth gave a touch of melancholy, of those poor coarse hands, all chapped and fissured, of those black nails and blue overalls.

'But, alas! I am now as I always was, a prisoner. I have not known how to free myself from myself so that I might give that self to you.

'Now, the old muddied past flows back upon me. Once again the bad days bear me company, and the sense of my selfish, envious mediocrity. All that I dreamed in that time of my illusions, the law of duty before which my will was determined to bend—Dear God! must all that sink and founder?'

XIV

THE comrades were gathered about Jérome's bed. He was due to go back to Paris in the course of the day. Passing through Bordeaux, after a pilgrimage to Lourdes, he had given a lecture on the previous evening. Vincent Hiéron, kneeling on the floor, was piously collecting the Great Man's underclothing, the flannels still damp from his profuse sweatings. For the Master had taught him that the humblest tasks have a grandeur about them when carried out for *the Cause*.

The others were devotedly gazing at their idol. No doubt, to anybody else he would have looked ugly, with that squalid, dirty ugliness which is to be seen on every man at the moment of waking, once he has left youth behind him. But his eyes had still the same fire, the same depth of tenderness and dreams—an irresistible attraction, and, in his smile, in the way he folded his arms behind his head, there was still something of adolescent grace, though he was close on thirty. It is as though time were unwilling to do more than lightly touch those who have kept their faith unsullied, who still retain the hope, the love, which was theirs when they were twenty. Do not the poets on whom the years lie heavy keep an eternal youth within their eyes?

'What's *your* name?' he asked a stocky young man who was gazing at him with the moist look of a faithful hound.

'Marteau.'

'Marteau! what a splendid name, and how well it suits you!'—and he laid a hand upon his back.

One who pursues the calling of an apostle is free from all the conventions. Jérome arrogated to himself the privilege of never being polite. Nor did anyone hold it against him. Quite unconsciously these young men had submitted to the influence of that rather crude Nietzscheism in which the world of to-day seems to feel itself at home. The Master was, for them, a sort of Superman. Besides, they said somewhat artlessly, speaking of themselves—*we belong to the élite*.

Jérome dipped a piece of toast in his chocolate.

'Is Georges Élie here?' he asked.

The young man in question stepped forward, blushing furiously, and hanging his head.

'Was it you sent me that letter to Lourdes about Jean-Paul Johanet? I have looked into the matter. You did well to warn me. He has been criticizing my articles, displaying bourgeois prejudices and the most stupid kind of irony.'

Then, addressing the whole company, the Master added in a solemn voice:

'Listen to me, my friends. There is among you an intellectual *poseur*, a dilettante who will be your ruin if you allow him to have the least influence. His name is Johanet.'

'A bourgeois!' muttered Georges Élie.

'My children'—continued Jérome: 'it is right and proper that, even when absent from you in the flesh, I should be present deep in the heart of each one of you. Within this flock there must be no will at variance with mine. My children, you are clean, but not all. . . .'

Was it deliberately that he made use of words like those of Christ? That he had done so occurred to none, and, even if it had, their encounter with Jérome Servet had been, for most

E

of those present tantamount, almost, to a meeting with God. There was upon his face a look of inexpressible anguish.

'Listen: for the welfare of the Bordeaux Group, it is essential that this Johanet be got rid of—essential. The wretched creature is coming here. You must accuse him in my presence. Don't be surprised if you hear me speaking gentle words to him. I must show no violence. . . .'

Jérome did not intend that his prestige should be diminished as the result of petty quarrels. Perhaps, too, he hoped that the miserable apostate would part from him without feelings of hatred. . . .

But Vincent, who was engaged in strapping the suitcases, clambered to his feet. He was scarlet in the face.

'O! Jérome, why all this play-acting?' There was something of contempt in the look which the Master directed at him. But just as he was about to reply, a knock came at the door, and Jean-Paul entered the room.

XV

Two hours later, in his bedroom, Jean-Paul pulled down the blinds. The abuse levelled at him by the comrades had been of unprecedented grossness. But the Master's artless treachery had appalled him. Yet what, really, did it matter? He felt no movement of rebellion against Jérome Servet. He was prepared to forgive that superb Hunter of Souls anything. What he now chiefly remembered was Vincent Hiéron drumming with his fingers on the window-pane, too cowardly to utter a word.

Jean-Paul wiped his eyes and took a hold on himself. The trivial sounds of the street died away in this room where he was gasping for breath. He could hear doors being shut, a child playing scales. No one anywhere was sparing a thought for *his* distress. Under the sagging weight of the day just past, he felt utterly alone, alone for ever, without purpose, without faith, without love.

He summoned memories to his aid. But at first the past appeared to him as no less empty than the present, and the tight little smile which, in imagination, he could see on Marthe's lips, brought him no comfort. Here, on the very brink of an abyss of loneliness, he felt giddy and wanted to die.

There was a metal cross standing on the table. In vain did he try to pray. Obedient to a habit acquired in his schooldays, he opened the Gospels at random—and read a passage which had no possible bearing on his situation. To this small incident he attached a quite extraordinary importance, and, looking at

the cross and at the small volume in his hand, he murmured:
'Is the whole thing just a tremendous lie?'

The blasphemy roused his heart to passionate protest. He
knew that at the least call for help, He, whom he had betrayed
at every moment of his life, would have opened wide His
arms. He was tempted to fall to his knees, to abandon himself
to the Infinite Being whose love remained, for him, a certainty
beyond the power of words to express, something stronger
than all his doubts, than all his negations.

But Jean-Paul wished neither to see nor to hear, and, because
his heart asked for no mercy, the Comforter withdrew from it.

The bells of the electric trams ceaselessly broke the silence of
the provincial street. Every object in the hotel bedroom took
on for Jean-Paul a strange and hostile look. Then, the light
began to drain away. A siren drove its mournful note through
the mists of the harbour.

The young man lit one cigarette after another—they were of
an expensive gold-tipped brand—and little patches of smoke
hung motionless in the air filling it with a smell which was like
that of the countryside when the peasants are burning weeds.

An unruffled melancholy, a desperate calm held sway over
Jean-Paul's heart. Opposite to him was the door, painted in
three different tones, and he found himself remembering the
day when Georges Élie had slammed it so violently.

'Poor boy,' he murmured: 'why should *I* blame you for
trying to see a friendship in terms of infinity—I, who, as a
schoolboy, knew so well those heavy, lingering dusks when
one cried for no cause, and the heart was pricked into wakefulness? Like you, I centred on one chosen friend all the un-
appeasable desire I felt for union, lest otherwise I die.'

He remembered how, on Saturday evenings, after confession,
they had managed to meet in the deserted playground.

Sparrows would be cheeping round crumbs left over from the boys' 'snacks', and, on the gravel, silver paper from bars of chocolate caught the light.

In the unsullied ignorance of their hearts, they fanned their exaltation with artless, passionate words: 'Tomorrow we will take Communion, each for the other,' Jean-Paul would say. They exchanged little sacred pictures.

In summer, when the last of the day-boys had gone home, the boarders had a recreation period before evening prayers. Jean-Paul's friend said: 'Point out Arcturus to me. I can never find the Little Bear. . . . Isn't that Cassiopeia?' He wanted to be a missionary, and was reading *les Annales de la Propagation de la Foi*. . . . 'We will travel in canoes on the Great Lakes . . .' but, 'No,' said Jean-Paul, 'I am going to be a great poet and write a book like *La Génie du Christianisme* which shall convert all France, after which, I am going to marry and have children. . . .' Then his friend would answer with a blush: 'We should not indulge in idle talk.'

Slowly the vision faded . . . and Jean-Paul became sharply aware of the burden of his poor and devastated heart. But was it not at hours such as this that the past sounded endlessly like the little waves of a calm sea? The broken heart sees no light on the horizon, and turns back to the forsaken shore where, one by one, like stars at evening, memories awake and shine.

Away in the silent building someone was playing the piano, though the sound came indistinctly to his ears. It brought him help. The silken hair of his small boy friend, the delicate outline of his face, vanished away, and, instead, he saw Marthe, so frail, so slender, with her heavy mass of hair. In those days, the small Jean-Paul had not yet developed that passion for analysis, that spirit of criticism, which would never leave him in peace, and, later, was to kill in him all friendship and all love.

During the hot summer holidays he had scarcely ever answered his friend's melancholy letters. He and Marthe and two other girls took sides in games of croquet. The vesper bells tinkled in the blaze of Sunday afternoons. They argued. . . . The rows of trees cast great velvety shadows across the grass.

He remembered one of those young girls with whom he had fallen in love shortly before the end of the holidays. She was now dead. She had taught him tennis. He had liked playing in shirts of a fine soft material, with the sleeves turned back from his wrists. She said to him: 'You've got arms like a girl'—'and you, like a boy'—he answered, ashamed of being always beaten. He could see her still, in her white piqué dress, a slim figure with well-developed muscles. He could hear her gusts of laughter, the words she used, words with two meanings, either very false or very artless, which made him blush; words that haunted him at night and kept him awake.

Two years ago, he had seen the tennis-girl for the last time. Her narrow iron bedstead had been wheeled out on to the terrace, but even so she seemed to breathe only with the greatest difficulty. Her hair was stuck to her pallid brow. Her father said: 'Go a little farther off, you might catch the infection.' For a while, she followed him with her eyes. . . . Did she know?—perhaps.

He remembered how her mother had embraced him with tears in the hall, and said: 'She was very fond of you.'

Once so imposing and so kind, she had grown suddenly old. Jean-Paul could still see her, on the great feast-days, in the village church, where her magnificent contralto voice was a source of considerable amusement to the country-folk. But Jean-Paul always cried when she sang Schubert's *Abschied*.

The piano was silent. The visions died away. Who now could wake again the innocent heart-throbs of youth? On this evening of pain and grief, he felt in himself the same old frustrated longing for love. But what face, what heart could resist successfully the cruel clarity of his mind? He could no longer love. Never had he suffered so intensely as now when every prop had buckled under him. He was obsessed by a phrase: *loveless under an empty sky*. The coarse laughter of men, the shriller laughter of women rose from the street. With bitter irony, Jean-Paul said to himself:

'There is always pleasure. . . .'

XVI

THERE was, at Castelnau, a cool retreat where Marthe's great-grandmother had spent her days.

Against the neutral-tinted wall-paper hung several amorous prints. 'I'm told they have some value'—said Monsieur Jules Balzon. The old lady's deep sofa was still in its place, and shepherds smiled at their shepherdesses in faded pink. A small set of shelves held a few books . . . the poems of Musset together with the same author's *Comédies et Proverbes*, the poems of Madame Ackerman, a curious first edition of *les Pleurs* by Marceline Desbordes-Valmore, *Atala* and *René*. The good lady who, half a century earlier, had lived in this remote corner of the country, must have shed many a tear over their impassioned pages. Her sensible great-granddaughter who, for a long time, had been careful not to read them, did at last make their acquaintance and exacerbated her unhappy love with the magnificent literature which they contained.

But when she heard her father's shuffling footsteps on the terrace, she quickly put away her book and sat down at the piano and sang, for herself alone, the *Dichterliebe*. . . .

One day, during luncheon, a letter arrived from Bordeaux. Monsieur Balzon studied the envelope, said: 'It's in Jean-Paul's hand,' and, while Marthe, with a beating heart shut her eyes, set himself, unhurriedly, to collect on the prongs of his fork a piece of steak, a little fat, a segment of potato—and waited until these varied items had soaked up the requisite amount of gravy. . . .

'Oh! do read it, father!'—Marthe exclaimed impatiently.

Monsieur Balzon neatly sliced open the envelope with his fruit-knife.

'Jean-Paul will be here tomorrow, and will spend one day with us before going on to his father. You will have a pleasanter companion than me . . .' then he added: 'he'll be at Castelnau every day, you see if he isn't, and the more the merrier. I like talking with that young man. I think he's interested in the work I'm doing on Lucile de Chateaubriand. But he finds me a bit of a bore.'

Marthe protested.

'Oh yes, he does . . . our likes and dislikes are so different. He despises all the writers I enjoy. He thinks Sully-Prud-homme unworthy of serious attention, and he laughs at François Coppée. He uses the word genius of books I don't understand, and mentions to me names I've never heard: Jammes, Claudel, André Gide. . . . He gets quite worked up over Barrès. The fact of the matter is, he thinks me an old fool.'

'No, really he doesn't, papa . . .' and Marthe gave the old gentleman a happy hug.

XVII

A ND now, here she was, walking in the twilight with
her beloved.
'What is it you want me to comfort you about?'—
she asked softly.

Jean-Paul felt touched by her eagerness to help.

'Let's sit down on this bench, Marthe: it's a good place for
talking.'

The bench was set against the trunk of a tree which was
popularly known as the 'great oak' though others near it were
much larger. The copse stopped short on the edge of meadows
which looked almost too green, and had the appearance of
being wet. Already, at six o'clock, the mist was hanging low
over them. The alders along the river bank, which had been
the delight of Jean-Paul's boyhood, had been cut back. But
they were fast growing again and already formed a leafy screen
across the meadow, hiding the river which chattered by,
invisible.

'Marthe—I have been trying to break out of myself—I
wanted to perform an act of renunciation . . . but the effort
did little more than prove my own powerlessness.

'I was never more completely prisoner of myself than during
that experience in the mission-field on which Vincent Hiéron
and Jérome Servet persuaded me to enter. Ah! those poor
young chaps to whom we think we are doing so much good!
All it really amounts to is giving their souls a temporary
tidying up. We turn them into something not unlike those

gardens created for a flower show, which last only for a few days. . . .

'When one young man comes across another young man who wants to save him, he ought to run for his life!'

'But did you not love their souls for their own sake, Jean-Paul? . . .'

'Can one ever feel love for a soul for any better reason than that one thinks one can get something for oneself out of that love? Those to whom one grows attached, saying to oneself: "Even Jesus had a beloved disciple", are destined to share in that long-drawn-out death which is the fate of all friendship, whether one hastens the end by discarding the object like a worn-out suit, or lets one's feeling degenerate into mere pity, in which case our kindly gestures are no more than lies without meaning. . . . What an agony it is either way!'

Marthe got up.

'It's getting cold,' she said.

The two young people took the path which led round the park. Marthe's dress was a patch of brightness in the dusk. Jean-Paul was thinking: 'What's the use of talking to somebody who doesn't understand? . . .'

But the girl suddenly murmured words which showed that she was still attentive.

'Your heart is as closed to friendship as it is to love!'

'That is true, Marthe: but do you know what love is?'

In a voice which she tried to make sound indifferent, she said:

'Yes, Jean-Paul, I do . . .'

He dared not answer, and slashed at the tall bracken with his stick.

The sound of a motor-horn ripped the air. The young people returned in haste. Monsieur Bertrand Johanet, looking enormous in his fur-coat, embraced the young man with shy affection.

'I couldn't wait till tomorrow, Jean-Paul!' His thick, ill-kempt beard revealed no more than a few inches of cheek tanned by sun and air. . . . His red, swollen nose shone like a live ember in his undistinguished face. Tufts of hair projected from his ears. The huge, bulky man seemed as embarrassed in the presence of his over-sensitive son as he had been in that of the young woman who had lived and died in his company, faithful, silent and resigned.

The dinner was long and plentiful. Jules Balzon adored his cousin. They had childhood memories in common which the professor brought vividly to life. . . . Jean-Paul's father laughed noisily, got very red in the face, and, when his son offered him a glass of water, said:

'That's very kind of you.'

XVIII

ALL through those blazing, empty days, Jean-Paul, much to his surprise, found that he had forgotten his pain. He had ceased to think. He became conscious of how young he was. In the turning upside-down of all his inner life, he suddenly discovered the possibility of leading a purely physical existence, in which love-making should be his only form of happiness.

It was but a short while since he had been filled with scorn for those vain and excessively elegant oafs whose only purpose in life seemed to be to attract the opposite sex. . . . It now began to occur to him that something of the same kind was all he had to look forward to. He excused himself for playing the animal on the specious ground of having wanted to play the angel. After the resentments and the treacheries which had reduced him to tears, the thought of a vague indulgence in passionate hungers brought him so great a feeling of relief that he was eager to see it crystallize round the first pair of charming eyes that should come his way—the first little soul he might discover in the precious envelope of a tempting body.

'Until this moment'—he thought—'I have been mine own executioner. . . . Ever since the age of fifteen my life has been nothing but a passionate struggle with solitude—from which I have always emerged the loser. What could I not have done if only I had been finally freed from the self-loathing bred of isolation? . . . I want to be like other men, finding a simple happiness in passion.'

No longer did he look on Marthe as the 'young girl, the incarnation of a pure and tender reasonableness'.

She, after over-indulgence in the books which she had found in her great-grandmother's library, had become soft and sentimental. When, in the early afternoons, they lay together on the warm sand of a bank, soaking in the sun, it scarcely worried her at all that he should approach his face to hers and amuse himself by tickling her forehead, her eyes and her lips with a blade of grass—to find out whom she 'loved the most'. It seemed to her that there was more of tenderness in his eyes than once there had been, and at the thought that perhaps he might love her, she felt faint with happiness. How should she have known that desire is not the same thing as love?

Jean-Paul might not love her, but it was true, all the same, that he felt something of a thrill when, at siesta time she lay beside him with her hands behind her head, revealing on her bodice odorous patches of sweat-stained linen.

But the imprudent young creature no longer kept a watch upon her words, and, while Jean-Paul lay dozing, gave voice to idle nothings and trivial bits of nonsense, so that he, barely listening, said sometimes to himself: 'She's just like every other young girl, a limited little creature with nothing in her mind beyond domestic chores.'

At dusk, after the passing of a storm, when the rain had brought a freshness to the air, he would set off alone along the 'sunset walk' which was the name they gave to the long avenue leading out on to the heath, towards the west.

How miserable he felt at those times! His thoughts turned to a youngster of eighteen, met one evening in the house of a

friend, who drank absinthe because he had read that it was
poison. The boy had said to him: 'When one has known the
last sensation capable of bringing one delight, it is time to die.'
Music, his sole source of happiness, could lead him to the
furthest limits of despair, and wake in him an overwhelming
desire to close his eyes for ever. . . .

'Ah!'—said Jean-Paul to himself; 'what was there to say to a
heart so young, so devastated? What, God apart, are all those
petty gods with which one encumbers oneself—tradition,
family, race, the dead?'

Each evening, the car came round to take Jean-Paul back to
his father's house. It was a sweet delight to him to feel himself
being carried through the darkness of the lonely roads. Smoke
rose gently from the crouching farmsteads. A light twinkled in
a window. Moonlight lay upon the humble sloping roof, the
bakehouse, the byres, the well. . . . Sometimes a cock woke up,
deceived by the brightness in the sky, and started to crow.
Jean-Paul remembered this same road at this same hour, when,
as a little boy with sleepy eyes, he used to sit dreaming in the
victoria. . . . As now, in those days, the moon pursued him
from tree to tree until the house was reached, and the un-
clouded sky showed like water between the black trunks of the
tall pines. 'It was just here,' his father would say: 'that your
grandmother was once chased by wolves.' He recognized the
heady scent of acacias, the warm reek of the cattle-sheds. . . .

He thought about that Paris life for which he so desperately
longed. He was appalled to find within himself a secret
craving to sink back into the slime. . . .

The car-wheels grated over the surface of the gravelled
drive. The lamp in the billiard-room shone harshly on to the
terrace where, in a wicker chair, Monsieur Bertrand Johanet
sat smoking his pipe. . . .

As was but natural, father and son stayed there for a while together. Monsieur Johanet spoke of practical matters—he had been offered such and such a sum for the Ousilanne timber; his shepherd over at Prat was dissatisfied with the sixty francs a year he was being paid . . . a lot of disruptive ideas were creeping into the countryside.

Martine, the cook, brought him his nightly 'grog'. He added rum to the mixture.

'Sure you won't have a drop, Jean-Paul? . . . nothing better for the stomach. . . . By the way, my boy, there's a letter for you—I'd almost forgotten.'

This he said cheerfully. Thanks to that blessed letter he wouldn't have to go on making conversation. He went back to his smoking and his sipping, for all the world as peaceful as the rumination of his cows two hundred yards away.

Jean-Paul recognized Vincent Hiéron's writing. This is what he read:

'Forgive me for having given you pain. . . . I believed that I was sacrificing you to *the Cause*. . . . I see now that I was needlessly cruel. . . . But I know you have so sweet a nature, and are so little given to harbouring a grudge that now, when great sorrow has come to me, it is of you that I find myself thinking. Since you left, Jérome Servet has grown suspicious of me. He has been listening to a lot of lying talk. Little Georges Élie, whom Jérome is taking to Paris to work on the paper (he feels no qualms whatever about uprooting these young provincials!)—little Georges Élie said to me the other evening —"Your reign's over!" How miserable to think that *Amour et Foi* is turning into a Court, with all its attendant intrigues, jealousies and plots. . . . But in my heart, Jean-Paul, I feel no resentment against the man who was the occasion of my being born again into the true life. . . .'

XIX

THE moths were fluttering round the lamp which Jean-Paul had just lit. He glanced for a moment through the window at a patch of night-sky, milky and lustreless as a dead opal. The stars which, at first, he had not seen, flashed out from the infinite spaces. Faced by those innumerable eyes, he felt the cry uttered by Jules Laforgue rise to his lips: *étoiles, vous êtes à faire peur.* Then he read his friend's letter through again, and sat down to answer it:

'I am back in the room of my childhood—it is as though the enveloping darkness which hides its ugly ordinariness, had done something to sweeten and ennoble it. The lamplight gives me a feeling of intimacy. I can almost imagine that I hear, out in the passage, the sound of myself playing as a little boy. Dear Vincent, have no regrets. Even if things had not turned out as they did, I should have left *Amour et Foi* of my own accord.

'I thought once that it would help me to get rid of the past. But all that has happened is that I have been caught up again by that old Jean-Paul who is incapable of sharing in the enthusiasms which you tried so hard to impose upon him. . . . It can't be helped. Some of us are born with a restless wish to do good to our brothers—others, with a taste for the delicious pleasure which comes from probing into the intricacies of human souls. . . . The first are of those from whom heroes are bred: the second should give up any attempt to turn themselves into missionaries—as I am resolved to do.

'Is it my fault that men exist to enchant rather than to torment me?

F
79

'In spite of everything, *Amour et Foi* has, in some sort, brought refreshment to my spirit which now, as always, clings to the old formula of the evening prayer. . . . It is still essentially "liturgical". . . . Each one of the great festivals of the Church sets it winging above those abysmal depths where lie its squalid desires and evil dreams. . . . On those days a true and unseen presence of Good hovers over my destiny. A host of confused aspirations—which I thought long dead—hum within me like bees in a swarming hive. Who knows?—a time may come when I shall remain permanently under the influence of the adorable mystery.

'Just at the moment, dear friend, I have found again only the grey years of my adolescence. I am without either purpose or happiness, but I do not greatly suffer. Humbly, I accept life as it is, and am resigned to carry on an endless duologue with the mediocrity who dogs my footsteps.

'Why should I try to rebuild an intellectual life for myself? I have several times made the effort, and always it has been unproductive. You see, it does not respond to anything very deep in me. The search for truth has not, in my case, any sense of fruitful urgency. I am not sure, unfortunately, that it even represents an intelligent curiosity. It's only that I should like to raise my poor understanding to the level of that on which the minds of my more gifted friends move.

'I realize clearly what a mediocre creature I am. Such superiority as I can claim to the general herd, costs me dear. All the books I read, all the music, all the pictures, that stir me, are so many brutal reminders of my complete incompetence.

'I am interested in temperaments . . . but really attractive temperaments are rare. Most of them seem to me to be like those second-rate acrobats who run about the stage of a Music-Hall, and silence the orchestra just so as to make the

audience realize how difficult what they are going to do is. . . .
I am an exacting collector burdened with a critical sense. But if
that critical sense is strong enough to spoil, for me, the universe
in which I am becoming lined and wrinkled, it is still too weak
to stifle those childish tears which, when I was at school, I used
to shed in the waning daylight of the four o'clock recreation
period.

'For anyone who, like me, has reached a point where he has
lost all belief that there exists a reason for continuing to exist,
life becomes a very complicated affair—especially if one has no
particular liking for any form of *relaxation*. Cards, billiards,
tennis are, none of them, of the slightest help to me. I am fond
of sweets and of certain forms of reading, but my stomach
suffers from the first—and I have read and re-read everything
which is capable of touching me at all deeply. . . .

'I have no longer any friends. . . . What has happened to
those of whom I was so fond in the days of my bitter, passionate youth? The ones I happen to meet nowadays on my
walks abroad, give me a wide berth, because my grin frightens
them. . . . But, in this heart of mine which I am now un-
burdening to you, *our* friendship, yours and mine, Vincent, is
still a living reality among the many dreams on which I have
turned my back, the illusions which are now long dead and
gone.'

Jean-Paul stopped writing. The damp grass in the sleeping
garden, the snow-white acacias, the roses on the balcony, the
forest resin, combined in the concoction of so strange, so
intoxicating a fragrance, that he shut his eyes. 'What I said,
Vincent, is not true,' he muttered: 'I have not wholly un-
burdened myself, nor do you know everything about me; not
the full extent of my despair, nor to what pleasures I now
stretch out my hands.'

XX

THE holidays moved onwards to their end. The great equinoctial gales moaned ceaselessly through the pines and across the tawny billows of the bracken. The first ring-doves, precursors of the pigeons, streaked the pale sky.

The figure of a little boy with the pale face of a far distant day, drew near to him, raising those candid eyes in which only the sky was reflected. He clasped those schoolboy hands, brown hands faintly stained with ink, and, perhaps, spoke to him those ancient canticles which, on the eve of each fifteenth of August, he and Marthe had sung together under the night sky, at the time of shooting stars. . . . *God of peace and love, light of light.* His grandmother had been living in those days—a sturdy, pious old lady at whose side, as a boy, he had kneeled. The jade beads on her bodice had hurt his forehead. She wore an amethyst cameo at her throat, and he had always thought that the antique and precious piece of jewelry looked good to eat. . . . Then, he would ask God to forgive him for allowing his thoughts to wander. He was convinced that the Creator of the universe would come down next morning into his child's heart, and that this should happen seemed to him divinely natural. And, since his soprano voice was still unbroken, and he figured as the school soloist, he sang with Marthe the canticles of his First Communion, the ones it was impossible to hear without crying: *Oh, awful Tabernacle. . . . Heaven is come down to earth. . . .*

Jean-Paul wanted to flee from these memories, so deeply feared, so truly loved. But they kept leaping out at him each moment of the day. The Angelus bells sounded just as they had done in the days of his childhood, in just such fading dusks. . . . The last languorous heats of late September awoke in the young man, as they had done in the boy, the sense of anguish which belongs to going to school for the first time—the feeling of terror on the threshold of an unfamiliar life.

XXI

JEAN-PAUL got out of the train at the Quai d'Orsay
station. The day was mild and lowering, the street full of
the terrifying bustle which he had always associated with the
first day of term. He noticed that Paris was plunged in darkness: the electricians were on strike. He thanked them silently
for having kept the city in harmony with his state of mind.

A cluster of flickering Venetian lanterns lit the faces of the
passers-by from below, making their chins and lips look green.
Lying back in his cab, he decided that he had better renew
acquaintance with Lulu, that dreary friend, compact of
nothingness, whom once he had staggered with his bombast.
'For me'—he thought; 'he will be a wonderful tutor in
depravity—with the help of that idiot I shall learn how to
grovel in the gutter.'

In a narrow room with a low ceiling a Gypsy orchestra was
frantically at work dispensing savage music. Gentlemen in
evening-dress were uttering little yelps while a dancer, more
apache than any real apache could be, was performing the Valse
Chaloupéc, whirling his partner's listless, supple body in circles.

Four waiters flung themselves on Jean-Paul and Lulu,
stripped them of their overcoats, and showed them a menu on
which the most insipid beverage was priced at twenty francs.*

'You'll stand champagne, dearie, won't you?'

A woman was standing in front of them and ogling them

*Then about 15s.

84

with appalling coyness. Jean-Paul looked at the monster, and was not fascinated. A line from La Fontaine seemed to him apt to the occasion:

Passez votre chemin, la fille, et m'en croyez. . . .

'You're going to get into trouble, if you aren't careful'—said Lulu.

But the creature moved away, casting to left and right the eyes of a famished she-wolf. . . .

'I can find verses to fit the most fantastic situations'—thought Jean-Paul who was for the moment enjoying a mood of self-satisfaction.

He had drunk two glasses of Mumm, and felt a craving for sublimity.

'Why are all these people making so much noise?'

'Because it amuses them.'

'That's where you're wrong, Lulu . . . it's because they're terrified of silence. . . . The idea needs working out, I can see all sorts of pleasing variations . . . as in Maeterlinck's *Trésor des humbles.*'

'You're a bit drunk, dear old man.'

'Not drunk, just satisfied . . . completely satisfied.'

Saying which, he at once felt sad. 'How unspeakably filthy it all is, Lulu! what music! Only to think that with the same notes Wagner. . . .'

'Oh, shut up!' exclaimed Lulu. 'This isn't the place to start philosophizing. . . . Take a peep at that woman over there—second to the right . . . pretty good-looker, eh?'

'Right as ever, my dear Lulu. . . . It's not *all* ugly. . . . There's a nice impressionist picture to be made out of this. Look at those burning eyes in the face of that gaunt female, starving under her make-up. . . .'

'The gypsies are pretty good here'—said Lulu, well pleased with himself.

'Yes, I love this music of niggers in rut. It keeps one from thinking—and what do we come here for, Lulu, if not to find a minor form of suicide? the joy of getting away from life for just a few hours?'

They ordered more champagne. Just then, everyone in the room started shouting a chorus of which they could hear only the first words—*Caroline . . . Caroline.*

'What are you looking at, Jean-Paul?'

'I'm looking . . . looking . . . at the small page-boy over there by the door. He's, I should say, about twelve. He is studying with a serious and almost contemptuous expression, the antics of all these yelling and prancing grown-ups . . .' —and Jean-Paul murmured: 'Does he go to confirmation class, does he say his prayers?'

'Shut up!'—said Lulu.

But Jean-Paul, with his eyes on the ceiling and an inspired look on his face, declaimed:

Très sérieux, vêtu de livré amarante,
Un enfant de douze ans porte les vestiaires,
Le seul grave parmi tous les hommes qui chantent . . .
Va-t-il au catéchisme et fait-il sa prière?

They went home at dawn. In the leaden light gangs of squalid street-cleaners were creeping along the walls. Heavy market-wagons passed them. At the corner of a street several men standing at a stall, were drinking soup. Little clusters were huddling round a brazier, their coarse, outspread hands lit by the flames.

Jean-Paul thought of all those who, at this very hour, were getting up in cold bedrooms.

'Poor servant-girls'—he said—'bundling themselves into their clothes to go to the five o'clock Mass.'

They crossed the Seine which was rolling its yellow waters under the leaden sky.

'Come back with me, Lulu'—begged Jean-Paul.

'Not on your life . . . it's time for bed. . . .'

Jean-Paul did not insist. He looked at Lulu whose face was livid. There were dark circles round his eyes, and a small indentation at one corner of his mouth. His tall body was huddled in a great-coat, and he was walking with a stoop.

Alone in the street, Jean-Paul obstinately refused to think.

XXII

JEAN-PAUL was dining at Weber's with Lulu and Lulu's 'friend', a tall, bony young woman called Lucile, with a face like a horse and the accumulated wisdom of ten years experience of the ways of the world. Jean-Paul was little better than a novice, and her conversation made him blush for the waiter. He did his best to laugh at the obscene running commentary to which the creature treated him, and, since she seemed to have a particular liking for amorous confessions, assumed a mysterious and knowing air.... But she kept up a constant bombardment of questions, and, in the end he was compelled to admit, with a hang-dog expression, that he had not got a mistress.... This she seemed to regard as a good joke, and used as an excuse for indulging in a number of not very flattering suppositions.

Then, in spite of his enjoyment of a Henry Clay, in spite of the crushing weight of the lady's foot on his evening pumps, in spite of *Ah! l'effet que c'te musique me fait!* which the gypsy orchestra was belching into the room—he was on the point of taking to his heels and, revived by the night air, going to Montmartre to mingle with the silent groups which would be kneeling in the great basilica till morning, there to expiate the crimes of the night just past.

But he stayed where he was, and even listened with some curiosity to the woman, who was saying: 'I've got a sister, ducky . . . twenty years old . . . I'll introduce Liette to you. . . .'

Jean-Paul had a terror of those lonely walks home through
the darkness, when he was brutally forced to look his destiny
in the face. On the Saint-Pères bridge he walked more quickly
because of the black water into which the street lamps threw
a trembling reflection—and because he was seized with panic
at the thought of *leaning giddily above the fascinating presence of
death.*

Before going to sleep he read a pitiful little letter which
Marthe had written to him: '. . . You no longer come here,
dear cousin, and I am sad. If you could see me now, you would
find me much changed. But I have come to love your favourite
books, Jean-Paul, and would no longer get on your nerves
with my endless embroidery. In my heart there is a pain which
never sleeps. I try to lull it by saying the poems you once
recited to me. . . . But it is as much alive in me as ever—and I
find everything boring and dreary except my dear anxiety. I
have forgotten how to pray. I go down on my knees, hide my
face in my hands, and try—but the lovely words stop dead at
my lips, like the tunes of that musical box which was already
so old when we were small, and you enjoyed so much for their
sadness.

'I have been made to see a lot of doctors because I don't eat
and am pale. When I look at my face in the glass it is white and
drawn. The knowledge that I am no longer pretty does
something to console me for your absence.

'All day long I wait for the evening to come. The girls in
the drawing-class say that I am a neurasthenic because I never
go visiting, and am never at home when they come to see me.
But a visit from you, Jean-Paul would do me good. I can bring
myself to say that, though I know that once this letter has been
posted, I shall cry with rage and pride, and bite my pillow.

'How peaceful and simple life was in the old days! Every

hour, when I was young, was so sweetly regulated—fine needlework, a few charities, a little music, the quiet companionship of friends, the whispering and laughter round the tea-table whenever a young man came into the drawing-room.

'What is killing me now, Jean-Paul, was already present in me then. But to be happy seemed so easy. . . . I thought I could hear happiness coming.'

Jean-Paul tore the letter up. He was surprised to find that it had scarcely, if at all, moved him. Its effect had been merely irritating. 'Have I *no* heart?'—he wondered, but decided that those who love us more than we love them, are always hard to endure. . . . 'She, at least, has got her love, whereas I have not got even that—just a few sentimental yearnings without any particular object. . . . Ah! dear girls, how I envy you for being in love with me!'

Then he tried to imagine what that Liette was like of whom Lulu's 'friend' had spoken.

XXIII

VINCENT HIERON turned out of the street where a shabby crowd was fighting its way through the frozen mud and the failing light. Since he had ceased to frequent Jérome Servet, Jean-Paul's room had become his only refuge.

'This morning, I wanted to have a word with Jérome,' he said: 'I was kept kicking my heels in the outer office, and even so didn't get my interview. Luckily, though, I did get a glimpse of him as he was leaving, and had a "Hullo!" for my pains, with which I had to rest contented.'

Jean-Paul was thinking of Liette, as he had seen her the night before . . . a little animal bursting with life. The smell of her scent was still in his nostrils. He didn't want now, to fill his mind with anyone but her, and resented being forced to put up with Vincent with his load of morose enjoyments.

'You must respect your fallen idol, Vincent.'

'Alas! I can do nothing now but wrap him in that "purple winding-sheet in which the dead gods sleep". . . .'

Jean-Paul could not help smiling. So, Vincent Hiéron had taken to quoting Renan!

'Forgive me, Jean-Paul, if I say that no matter what Jérome may or may not do, he is still the Master to whom I owe the better part of myself. . . . There are many who will be saved simply because he one day crossed their path. . . .'

Jean-Paul said nothing. He passionately longed to be alone, and was overjoyed when his friend left him. Now, at last, he would be able to write to Liette. He had been waiting for this moment with that pleasurable sense of anticipation which old 'regulars' of the Opera-Comique feel when they eagerly look forward to hearing once again the letter-song in *Manon* or in *Werther*.

For Jean-Paul pieced together his love from odds and ends of literary memories. This artificial passion provided him with material for sonnets, and kept him lingering over well-composed missives. The poor girl was guilty of a number of blunders which, to some extent, spoiled the charms with which her friend's imagination had endowed her. She had a formidable rival in the imaginary Liette, the 'Liette-in-herself' over whom Jean-Paul brooded sentimentally in his lonely room.

That Liette, like Ninon de Lenclos, had something of the philosopher in her make-up, as well as the flexible graces, and the scruples of those high-born heroines who haunt the pages of Paul Bourget. She was a little animal, with the inherited melancholy of her kind: a yielding and tormented Bérénice.

But the flesh-and-blood Liette had, at least, this advantage over her rival, that she possessed a supple and wiry little body—slim legs that clung and twined like ivy.

Jean-Paul could not free himself from the fear that he did not really love her. 'I am twenty-three'—he reflected: 'and I have never yet felt anything that can be called love. My heart, it seems, is equally balanced between the wish to love and the inability to experience love. . . . Yet, when I resigned myself to living like other men, seeking the same pleasures, was it not of love that I was dreaming? Can I remain content with the small change of physical pleasure?'

Pictures formed in his imagination from which he had to turn away his eyes in disgust.

A clock struck four. The window-pane was running with water, like a tear-stained face, and already the street-lamps were springing into life. 'Thou has made me an exile, O Lord!'—he murmured—'an exile even from the world of human love.'

XXIV

To Jean-Paul's generosity Liette owed a fourth-floor flat in Passy, a maid and a cook. These two underlings performed an essential function in her existence. Jean-Paul was kept punctually informed of all their doings, and knew every detail of 'the girl's' insolent behaviour, and the gossip that was retailed in the local dairy-shop about her.

Jean-Paul had noticed, even in the discreet Marthe, that female curiosity about what 'the servants say'. Nothing else, he had decided, really interested women.

But even more than Liette's conversation did he dread the parties organized by Lulu, his friend, and a handful of casual acquaintances in the 'pleasure-haunts' of Paris, *artistic* cabarets and night-clubs where a synthetic happiness is concocted from champagne, a great deal of electric light, Gypsy music and 'apache' dancing. All through those dreary hours he spent the time remembering the quiet and solemn evenings that had once been his.

Oh! those evenings! He could see again in memory the close circle of a few intimate friends, when, despite the lateness of the hour, no one could bring himself to leave the warm little study, the small circle of lamplight, but each had picked from Jean-Paul's shelves some favourite book, and all had read aloud in turn.

An elegy by Francis Jammes held the sadness of old, deserted gardens haunted by the melancholy shades of those who once had been young girls, pupils of the Sacré-Coeur. It brought to mind dark country drawing-rooms where, in the torrid heat of the siesta, the whispering of the long grasses could be heard outside the windows.

Baudelaire's *l'Invitation au voyage* thrilled the young captive hearts on the threshold of a pure and ardent adolescence.

Then, someone—ah! how clearly could Jean-Paul hear his voice in these ignoble places—would murmur the ineffable music of Verlaine: 'Souvenir, souvenir que me veux-tu?' . . . and all the mystic ardours of *Sagesse* drooped to a dying silence. And when, at last, the spirits of his guests had reached the topmost peak where words seem vain and empty, one of them would sit down at the piano. What agony it was, amid the frenzied din of a Gypsy orchestra, to conjure up the assuaging chords of the *Moonlight Sonata!* . . .

Sometimes the casual companions of his 'pleasure' would turn serious. The women were silenced. The talk turned on aviation. One had no use for anything but monoplanes. Another demonstrated the inferiority of the Germanic race, basing his conclusions on the failure of the Zeppelins. There was one evening when they went so far as to discuss sociological problems.

Lulu, who had got through eighty francs' worth of *extra dry* in the course of the evening, said—'if the workers would save their money instead of spending it on drink. . . .'

Why was it that Jean-Paul remembered a certain evening in Bordeaux, when he had strolled with Vincent in the Public Gardens? A band was playing the march from Tannhäuser. There, in the heart of the great city, the smell of new-mown hay was heady, and the fragrance of the limes seemed to hold the deadly sweetness of monstrous flowers which lull, and kill. . . .

In the squalid cacophony of a Montmartre night-club, he

G

recalled those hours of exaltation in the quiet alleys of the Public Garden in a provincial town. . . . He heard again Vincent's voice giving him a piece of detailed information: 'In the Nord Department, Jean-Paul, a working-man with four children has had to apply for Poor Relief!'

He looked at the bestial faces round him. Liette's pink little hand—which had only recently begun to show the effects of manicure—was lying on the table. . . . At least he would not profane his feeling of despair—the only pride he still retained—by staying on in this ghastly den with all these degraded animals . . . then, he drank a glass of champagne, and Liette said:

'Jean-Paul's beginning to get gay. . . .' And gay he was, and no mistake! With his two fists he beat out the rhythm of the apache dance on the table.

XXV

J EAN-PAUL leaned for a moment on the parapet of the
Saints-Pères bridge, as though drawn thither by the black
water in which there lay the trembling reflections of the
lamps. With a gesture which had become habitual with
him, he drew his fingers across his face. They still smelled of
musk and Turkish tobacco.

Liette's sensuality now did nothing but exhaust him and fill
him with disgust. The time had come to flee from it. But,
with that gone, what had he left?

Three o'clock struck. Paris seemed as though suddenly
deserted after some great disaster. He was alone. How was he
going to spend the day? There was nothing in particular to
occupy him.

Oh! to sleep . . . to sleep for ever! Leaning there above the
darkness of the river, he summoned up courage to say—to die!
Terrified, he moved away from the parapet.

Slowly he climbed his night-bound staircase, fearful of
finding himself in his cold and lonely room . . . or, perhaps,
indifferent to everything, no longer even feeling that vague
desire to get home which always made him hasten. . . . So
great a weariness lay upon him that, on the second landing he
had to stop, pressing both hands to his heart.

To himself he said: 'Why am I afraid of death?—it is not
the momentary agony of the last gasping breath that makes
me recoil. Is it God I fear?'

That single word, uttered in a tone of irony, overwhelmed him. He said aloud: 'Is it you, my God, whom I fear?'

He felt the tears come into his eyes. It seemed to him suddenly as though there were within himself the sense of an infinite something, as though He whom he had always thought so distant had never been so close to him as now . . . salvation had come to him in the awakening of his religious consciousness.

Was he just yielding to it with the shrewdness, the ability which he had always had, to fabricate emotions, to deceive himself while, at the same time, remaining sincere? No. At this moment, of all the petty dodges learned from books, nothing remained.

'When you think that you are far from me, it is often, then, that I am closer to you that I ever was.' Of this phrase, so charged with love, he could hear the echoes sounding through the silence of his heart. The mysterious activity of Grace! Through all his sad, tormented life, the young man had often felt God pouncing suddenly upon his heart as on a prey. How often had not that crashing thrust of goodness held him motionless upon the very brink of some unutterable foulness? For a moment, he stood quite still, panting, like a man who has just escaped from some tremendous danger. . . .

He kneeled down. On the table, among piles of books, gleamed a little metal Christ—a hideous object which had been given to him on the occasion of his First Communion—but which he revered because, in times of fever, it had known the tears and kisses of his early youth.

'O Lord!'—he murmured: 'before I could return to you it was necessary that all my props should be shattered. After having crossed, in vain, the threshold of degraded pleasure, my wretched heart, at last, is swallowed up in You . . . for nothing remains to me, unless it be You, into whose arms, this night, an instinct of self-preservation has flung me, muddied and soiled, but weeping. . . .'

Now, on this high peak of emotion, he did not force his voice. The whole of his Christian childhood was singing within him. Tears poured from his eyes, and he stammered broken words:

'O you, pain, of which I longed to die, it is you that now will be the reason for my living. . . . O rapture of suffering that brings me love! . . . O tears, which shall wash my sullied heart and cheeks, and all the souls that I have smirched. . . . O wounds! O bruises! which shall make me liker to my God! . . . O loneliness of heart, of which I was slowly dying, O terrifying silence of my solitude, which has made it possible for me to hear the impassioned summons of my Saviour, how I bless you now! What must I do to keep you?'

He opened the window. A party of men was in the street. They were shouting an obscene chorus which he recognized. He remembered that his fingers still smelled of musk and Turkish tobacco. 'Pleasure . . . pleasure . . .' he muttered: 'hideous music, painted women, diseased and bestial, alcohol and smoke, gloomy couplings . . . to think that I should abandon You for all that, deny You, crucify You. . . .'

Up in the sky which was already growing pale, a bell tinkled.

'I am thinking of you, poor, young assistant priest in some Parisian parish, on your way, this morning, to say Mass for the servant-girls, children of Mary; you who will walk through foetid sickrooms, and, when noon is past, will wear yourself out in some coarse and noisy Boys' Club; who, after five o'clock, will be in the confessional, suffocated by the stinking breath of old women; who, when at last you go back home, at dusk, worn-out, sad and lonely, will get a workman's foul abuse flung in your face. . . .'

The bell had stopped. Jean-Paul set himself to meditate, to be present in the spirit at the early Mass.

'O little priest!'—he thought: 'over whose like Saint-Francis of Assisi wept; when, at night, you moisten the Saviour's feet with tears the world knows nothing of, may God pardon, because of you, the cowardly moans, the useless tears of voluptuaries like me. . . . With all your secret agonies you nourish the greatest of all loves. . . .'

The livid light of early dawn came into the room with a chilly breeze. Jean-Paul closed the window. Little by little his enthusiasm waned. But he still clung to his mood of exaltation, saying in his heart: 'O God! is it Your will that I should wear the threadbare, shiny, poor soutane of those who exhaust themselves in Your service by living their lives out in the slums? Or is it Your will that I should sacrifice myself in a Trappist silence for the sins of the world, for *my* sins?'

He stopped. He no longer felt any emotion, but only a crushing weight of weariness. Sleep would not come to him. 'I will arise,' he thought, 'and go to my Father. Because my fervour is abated, I must devote myself to pious practices, put "the penny in the slot", and hope that God will speak to me. . . .'

A look, a smile, still floated in his memory. She who loved him with a love so shy, so remote, so humble; she, who asked only to serve him; she, whose gentle reason had been, so often a light to his feet—Marthe, moved in and out of the dreams which flitted through his half-waking sleep. . . . 'Sad little heart'—he said to himself—'and the less good for having loved me. . . . How flat and feverish that letter was she wrote me. All the bookishness which, in the old days, she so much despised, has now become for her fuel with which to feed her love. . . . I leave nothing behind me but ruins.' Marthe, Georges Élie—he could not rid his mind of those two names, could not banish from his sight the two faces which he had marked with pain, drowning, because of him, their eyes in tears.

'I have played with their immortal souls, and that, O Lord! is the unpardonable sin. . . .' He recalled the words of the Sermon on the Mount: 'If ye love them which love you, what merit have ye? for sinners also love those that love them.'

'O Lord! even that I have not been able to do. I have not loved those that love me. . . .' He wept silently, his face pressed to his pillow. The storm burst over the dry and arid ground. A passionate desire to give himself, to love without hope of reward, took hold on him.

Seven o'clock sounded. He got up in haste and hurried to the church of Saint-François-Xavier. In the darkness of a confessional-box he cast off all his weaknesses, striking his head against the varnished wood in an access of penitence. When he rose from his knees he felt calmer, scarcely any longer troubled by delicate scruples and sins only ill-defined. Several old women in black bonnets were grouped about an altar where Mass was just beginning. Servant-girls were telling their beads with a sort of greedy concentration. Ladies with smooth, white faces were slowly drawing off their silken gloves. A sordid, faded creature whose task it was to hire out chairs, moved from behind a pillar. The pennies clinked in her hand.

XXVI

ONSIEUR Bertrand Johanet was waiting for the
coming of one of the day's chief pleasures—his
bowl of *café au lait*, and the slices of black bread
spread with salted butter. The rain was streaming down the
window. The mist-shrouded trees were scarcely visible.
Martine was fussing up and down the kitchen, a black kerchief
tied about her head. She no longer had any teeth. A beaky nose
between two round eyes gave her the look of an old hen. A
stale smell exuded from her person, the smell of plates off
which one has been eating eggs and fish. It was a matter of
pride with her that she had been born and bred on the estate,
and she respected Monsieur Johanet because he was rich. She
knew that a well-furnished table is the outward and visible sign
of wealth. She still remembered the year, and even the day,
when her pullets had been under-cooked, and she had forgotten
to singe the pigeons. 'How fond you must be of this stretch of
heath where you have always lived,' Marthe sometimes said
to her. 'Why yes,' was the answer: 'especially now that the
wood is fetching such good prices. . . .'

A bitch and two dogs were curled up as near as they could
get to the fire. On the table was a woodcock which Monsieur
Johanet had just shot. He was describing the incident slowly,
and with a wealth of detail.

'I noticed that Stop was pointing . . . we were in the ride
which skirts the old bit of marshland, just where there's a lot
of gorse. I crept forward—heard it take wing . . . vrr . . .

upped with my gun, and, Bang! . . . got it. . . . But you're not listening!'

'I've something better to do'—grumbled Martine—'Monsieur Balzon and Mademoiselle Marthe'll be here any moment now. . . .'

She was carrying the bowl of *café au lait*—it was almost as big as a soup-tureen—and, so as not to make a mark on the table, carefully set it down on last year's calendar. For Monsieur Bertrand Johanet, who had a private income of fifty-thousand francs,* and was free-handed, saw no point in throwing money away. . . . He cut his buttered bread into small pieces with which he filled the bowl. In the old days, Marthe and Jean-Paul had always enjoyed watching the big man at his breakfast. Stalactites of coffee hung from his moustache and beard. . . .

'A funny idea, and no mistake, for they Paris folk to come here for the New Year!'—said Martine.

'It appears that Marthe is suffering from anaemia. The doctor thinks she needs fresh air, and it's more sheltered here than at Castelnau.'

'What that young woman needs,' declared Martine sententiously, 'is a husband.'

She took a look at her stewpans and her roast. They were to have for lunch a dish of cold, assorted meats, a leg of mutton, a hare, and a *purée* of woodcock.

'Better have the paté de foie, too. . . . I can hear the car . . . they've come.'

Marthe took off her furs and went to the fire. She seemed to be feeling the cold.

'You need fattening up, my dear,' said Monsieur Johanet, and Martine added:

*£2,000 p.a. in money then and much more in real value.

'She's all eyes.'

It was true that her light-coloured eyes appeared to have grown larger. Her tawny hair seemed to hang like a weight in the nape of her neck.

'I'm afraid of losing my rings,' she said. The little gold hoop which she had worn since her First Communion, was now too large for her finger.

She went upstairs and Monsieur Johanet settled down with his cousin in the smoking-room.

The air was stale with the reek of old cigar-smoke. On the walls were photographic enlargements by Nadar, of Monsieur Johanet's parents, and a relief-map of France by the Geographer to His Majesty the Emperor. It was here that Monsieur Johanet received his labourers, listened to their grievances, and paid them, because he knew they liked it, in five-franc pieces.

'Do you find Marthe changed?' asked the Professor.

Monsieur Johanet pressed down the burning tobacco in his pipe with his thumb, and muttered with some embarrassment:

'Shall I tell you what Martine says?—she says the girl needs a husband. . . .'

Monsieur Balzon flushed. 'I could ask nothing better, Bertrand. . . .'

The two cousins exchanged a smile. 'Two minds with but a single thought, Jules.'

'They'd make a handsome couple,' said Monsieur Balzon, '. . . and they should have their million to set up house with.'

Monsieur Johanet looked worried.

'I don't know what plans Jean-Paul has made. . . . A nice lad, a well-brought-up lad, but he's read a lot of books. He's a scholar, you know, a poet. . . . I feel as awkward with him as I would with a stranger. . . .'

'That's a sad state of affairs'—said the Professor in a low voice.

Jean-Paul's father made one of those gestures by which country-folk indicate that nothing can be done. It's just that things are like that. . . . The young and the old never really understand one another.

He got heavily to his feet, and, with a marked stoop, went across to his desk. From it he took a photograph, and looked at it in silence.

'You know, Jean-Paul's the very image of his mother. I've never known what goes on in his head any more than he knows what goes on in mine.'

The photograph trembled in his large, hairy hands. . . .

In what was almost a whisper, he said: 'But that doesn't make me any less fond of him.'

Monsieur Balzon, with his elbows on his skinny thighs, poked the fire. He could see by the light of memory two young women in the park, reading aloud the Comedies of Musset and the novels of George Sand. When the Professor went back to Paris, they wrote to one another every day. . . . Professor Balzon remembered an evening when his wife had caught him reading one of these letters. She had expressed her indignation in highly melodramatic terms.

'Try to find out what are Jean-Paul's views. . . . I'll have a word with Marthe.'

'We'll have grandchildren yet, Jules—and I'll give them their first guns.'

XXVII

MARTHE sat dreaming in the great bedroom where Martine had left her. On the table stood a water-jug of really startlingly pink glass—'Easter-egg colour', Jean-Paul used to call it. The upholstery and hangings had a pattern of little bunches of flowers. The thick woollen coverlet on the bed gave off the sort of smell one finds in country cottages. The top of the long mirror had a picture on it representing a mill with ducks, a woman doing her washing, and a man driving two large red oxen. For Marthe and Jean-Paul these figures had had a mysterious life of their own. The two children had invented names for each of them. Marthe remembered that they had called the peasant and his wife Monsieur and Madame Colorado—though why, nobody knew.

The light in this room was still as dull and drab as it had always been. It gave the young woman, though she was barely twenty, a terrible sense of the passage of time, of a remorseless movement towards the grave—of something being killed by every fleeting moment.

Her father had spoken to her of Jean-Paul. She had said nothing that could have revealed her feelings, had even begged that he should not be written to. . . . She felt that uncertainty was preferable to knowledge, since it still left a small margin of hope. If Jean-Paul had answered 'no', how could she ever have found strength enough to live?

She felt herself suddenly invaded by a great flood of cowardice. She would rather die, she thought, than hear the fate in store for her. She opened the window. The night air felt icy on her shoulders. So deep was the silence that she could hear the sound of the stream running over its sandy bed and the long mossy weeds. The cold air was like a burning wound in her breast.

'Day follows day,' she thought. They would have to go back to Paris. It was clear to her that one cannot take leave of life as one walks out of a room where one is feeling bored. She still carried about with her the image of Jean-Paul. But his features had somehow disappeared, and the light had gone out of his eyes. She could no longer see him distinctly . . . not even when she let her eyelids droop, and left the work she was doing neglected in her lap. . . . The pain woke again and gnawed at her only when Monsieur Balzon started to speak of a serious-minded young man, the son of a rich and honour-able father, who was seeking her hand in marriage. . . . She fled for refuge to her room, locked the door, flung herself on the bed, and surrendered to grief as to some secret delight.

Monsieur Balzon grew resigned to the thought of a future in which his daughter would never leave him. Once again an air of sad tranquillity hung about Marthe's room. There were cushions to be embroidered for a charity-sale, and there was music: The *Moonlight Sonata*, the *Appassionata*, the *Chanson triste* and the *Invitation au voyage* by Duparc, to which Jean-Paul never grew tired of listening. There were the girl-friends whom she loved—the only outlet for her feeling of affection which she could find in all the world. Best of all, there was the Lady Chapel at the day's end, the Tabernacle before which all the love of her poor heart could pour itself out. . . . Marthe had given up waiting for anything to happen. She merely went on living.

XXVIII

J EAN-PAUL whose heart had once leapt when anyone rang
at his doorbell; Jean-Paul who used to live in a state of
constant expectation, now drugged himself with solitude.
He fled in terror from the places and the persons who
reminded him of the life which, till then, he had been living.
He went far out of his way to avoid certain streets. He would
turn sharply on his heel when a familiar face smiled at him
from a distance, or when a close-fitting little hat suddenly
glimpsed, looked as though it might be the one which over-
shadowed Liette's restless eyes.

Only Vincent Hiéron was received with pleasure in his
small fifth-floor flat. Like all the young men who had been
caught up in the *Amour et Foi* Movement, Vincent felt a strong
desire to give himself to missionary work, and, with the
intention of doing so, had marked the day on which he
attained to his majority, by leaving an excessively frivolous
mother, basing his decision on a passage in the Gospel:
Whosoever shall love his father or his mother more than me . . .
and in this way had escaped from the empty social existence
to which he had been stupidly condemned.

He lived on money which he had inherited, and on what he
could earn by journalism. His room, a huge cell-like place with
a flagged floor, was very cold. It was situated in the rue des
Reservoirs at Versailles, in an old house which had once been
inhabited by La Bruyère. He was on terms of intimacy with
the third assistant-priest of his parish, and occupied himself, in

a rather vague fashion, with social work. The vast ambitions of *Amour et Foi* were no longer enough to satisfy him. What he now set himself to do was to make contact with individual souls. Just now, he was much concerned over Jean-Paul's. That young man, acting on his advice, was still 'putting pennies in the slot', but there was a complete absence of fervour or of joy in his efforts.

The two friends had decided to make a retreat, with several former Vaugirard pupils, at a Jesuit house in the neighbourhood of Paris. A raw Spring gave a cold, bluish look to the over-tended garden in which atrocious statues of the Sacred Heart, the Virgin, and the numerous saints of the Jesuit calendar, stood flaking and peeling at every bend in the paths.

But oh! how Jean-Paul loved the evening Benediction! . . . From that gathering of youth upon its knees rose the *O Salutaris* and the *Tantum ergo* which he could never hear without being reminded of the light, sweet-smelling school-chapel of his early years. A young man swung the censer, and the smoke seemed to drown the altar with its unflickering candle-flames. Then, before the Infinite Presence, the congregation joined in the simple evening prayer. Jean-Paul listened once again to the old formularies of devotion, with which he had been familiar in childhood: *Knowing not whether death may come to me this night, into Thy hands, O Lord, do I commend my spirit.* How, when he was a child, had his heart contracted when the mystery of death was thus evoked.

House of Gold, Ark of the Covenant, Gate of Heaven, Star of the Morning, pure invocations of the soul in a state of Grace, rising to the rose-decked feet and smiling face of the Virgin, echoes from his own far-distant past. He could remember how he used to doze through the first prayers, the feeling of joy with which he started awake after the litanies; the few silent seconds during which one made pretence of examining one's conscience. . . .

When Jean-Paul communicated these impressions to Vincent, the latter grew indignant, and poured out upon him a preacher's eloquence.

'Just unadulterated emotionalism, Jean-Paul, self-indulgence pure and simple. You're just the same old dilettante who won't make a definite choice or commit yourself. You have always wished to live a thousand lives, to neglect no source of enthusiasm and exaltation. As a Catholic, you have found yourself immersed in a pagan society, and, seated at a banquet where all the luxuries and pleasures of the world are proffered, have, nevertheless, claimed for yourself the sacred heritage of a Christian childhood. . . . *But no man can serve two masters.* Is it not *that* truth which now torments you? You cannot escape from it: it holds you prisoner. . . .'

On the first evening, in his cell, Jean-Paul said to himself: 'You must be resigned to not being of the world; to not being known to those who live in it . . . you have made your choice.'

Then, he had opened his window and seen Paris in the distance, asleep under its pall of smoke. From somewhere nearby a contralto voice had reached his ears, and he had recognized Schubert's *Junges Mädchen.* Then, he had thought of Marthe, and had decided that the duty which demanded his adherence was the most ordinary, the simplest, most commonplace in all the world.

For three days the preacher prevented him from coming to terms with himself. But, at least, in that luminous and naked Spring, he could taste the sweetness of thinking about Marthe, about that far-away love in which he felt his heart enveloped. Each day he wrote a letter which the girl received with a small

quiver of delight. Jean-Paul was not unaware of the pleasure
he was giving. He liked to think of Marthe, at midday, waiting
at the door for the postman. 'She recognizes my handwriting
. . . she tucks my letter away in her bodice, and all through
lunch her fingers feel through the muslin the envelope she has
not so far opened. . . .'

He was careful, at first, not to speak to her of love, but to
confine himself to relating the simple incidents of his day-to-
day life: 'The preacher uses such ridiculously bombastic
language, that it is impossible to be moved by what he says.
To make matters worse, he has refurbished a stale panegyric
on the subject of Jeanne d'Arc which he had by him, and hands
out great slabs of it to us. This place is ideally suited to en-
courage the virtue of patience. The garden is very small, but
the paths are so arranged that they twist, turn and constantly
intersect, and, far away, on the horizon, lies Paris behind its
screen of smoke. The forest is close at hand, a world of leaves
and birdsong. The solemn faces of my young companions are
pleasant to look at, and, though the preacher is only so-so, we
have long periods of silence, and real solitude. . . . The meals
are a distraction. These Jesuits serve us with good, clean food,
though not very digestible, and the sauces are heating to the
blood. The use of our brothers, the vegetables, is more
honoured in the breach than in the observance. . . .'

On the third day, Providence so contrived matters that a
cold in the head interrupted the preacher's course of instruction.
His place was taken by another of the Fathers, whose spare and
simple eloquence had a profound effect upon his young
listeners, and held their attention. A more solemn note began
to sound in Jean-Paul's letters:

'My dear child: these last few days have been an astonishing
experience. My time has been spent in the silence of an un-

H

familiar house, broken only at intervals by the voice of a priest who forces me, without any beating about the bush, to face the actuality of my destiny. All he says has forced to the surface that moral destitution which I have been carrying about with me in the secret corners of my being. All sound ceases, and I am become like a valley in which the mists have suddenly been dispersed. Ah! it needs a God to ransom us, because, in spite of our tears, the acts we have committed cannot be as though they had never existed, since their evil consequences flow logically from them. What can we do, unaided? God alone can intervene, and, therefore, we must give more time to prayer. . . .'

With each day that passed he came to know himself better, and what he discovered frightened him.

'Marthe, I have been guilty of that false justice of Pilate of which Pascal speaks. I may not have been a declared enemy of God, but the unbelievers, seeing Christians in my image, must have a very poor idea of a religion which can produce such unworthy disciples! I have never really put into practice any doctrine other than that of paganism. Endowed with money, I have played the part of the bad rich man who lives far removed from his brothers in a world of facile and abundant luxury. I have a brain, but have undertaken only such tasks as have pleased me, and pleasure has been my sole concern. I have had friends, but have used them only for my own delight—as mere objects—immortal souls which I might have done something to save! Thus, my life has been nothing but a long-drawn-out hypocrisy. I have even managed to avoid that punishment which waits on sin—contempt. I am esteemed, imitated perhaps, admired and loved. Within me and without, I have been forwarding the work of death. None has passed sentence on me, save, perhaps, some poor and starving human soul, left, after passing contact with me, in a worse confusion than it was before. . . .'

Then, this especial terror diminished in sharpness. Jean-Paul, among the flowerbeds bright with jacinths, tasted of the peace promised by the Master to those who truly love Him. 'Marthe, I have found a sweetness in this Rule which hour by hour subjects me to the necessity of meditation, in this mechanism which inevitably leads one on from good works to works of piety. . . .'

He was surprised to find how much pleasure this correspondence gave him. One evening, much to his astonishment, he found himself clasping Marthe's photograph to his heart. On his knees before the open window which framed a space of sky drenched with moonlight, he felt that, in spite of all his spiritual poverty, he was yet a privileged being, and knew that, for him, the divine Grace had taken on the form of human love.

XXIX

I N that marvellous Spring, he went to live at Versailles
with Vincent Hiéron.

Each morning he would go alone to the Grand Trianon.
Unshuttered now, the peristyle seemed to be waiting to be
decked for some noble festival. Jean-Paul conjured up against
that background and in that light the sumptuous brocades of
the Venetian masters, and filled the steps with musicians
sitting over their instruments, tall greyhounds, and squatting
pages intent upon their games of dice.

He imagined one of them leaning against a column, his face
turned to the garden. In vain did women dance before him
swathed in mysterious veils, or his best-loved friend proffer a
brimming goblet, pointing to the empty place beside him.
The young man judged all these pleasures trivial. Wearied
of tender sentiments, he dreamed of other joys, another
love. . . .

Just so did Jean-Paul like to see himself. He wandered along
the symmetrical avenues. Old Virginia lilac-trees, with gnarled
trunks, stood at the corners of the wide lawns, like unmoving
censers. He crushed to his face the heavy clumps of violet
blossom. In the evening he leaned on the terrace which over-
looks the great canal. No one, at that hour, was moving there
except some silent gardener. From far away came the deep
rumble of the city's life, making still greater the joy of being
away from it. The air was rich with a medley of scents. An
invisible dove cooed gently in its dark world of leaves. Among

the clipped hedges stood the lovely music-room. He walked
among the sweet-smelling bushes and the rose-trees. He feared
to think of Marie-Antoinette, of the sickly verses of Albert
Samain. He wanted to forget that the boots of Bonaparte had
trod those paths.

Marthe wrote, urging him to come to Castelnau. 'I do not
know,' she told him, 'in whom to confide the secret of my
happiness. Father spends all his time with Lucile de Chateaubriand, and, when he sees me looking feverish, urges me to
seek serenity in the company of Great Men. He has put upon
my table the lives of Beethoven and Michael-Angelo by
Romain Rolland, as well as a *Lord Byron*. But I am too much
interested in myself to get excited over dead and gone passions.
My own are enough for me, and, lying in the grass which is
already tall and thick, I dream unceasingly of us. . . .'

Jean-Paul was pleased to know that he felt a lively wish to
be with Marthe again.

Once more they knew the empty, blazing holidays, the
hours of siesta spent side by side in the oppressive heat, the
monotonous sameness of the days, broken sometimes by the
breathless urgency of tocsins spreading from one village to the
next. They loved the pungent smell of burning resin when
through the pines the sky showed red and smoky.

With the oncoming of dusk, the two young people were
surprised to rediscover in themselves all the emotions of their
childhood. On the eve of the fifteenth of August their voices
joined in the same old-fashioned and impassioned canticle
which had moved them so deeply at the time of their First
Communions. They looked for, and they found, the same star
in the same swaying tree-tops.

One evening, Jean-Paul, turning the leaves of *The Life of
Lord Byron*, found and read aloud to Marthe a cry uttered by

the English poet: '*It was one of the deadliest and heaviest feelings of my life to feel that I was no longer a boy. . . .*'

'Ah! Marthe, in that I recognize all of myself! . . .'

They no longer, as when last they had spent the holidays together, indulged themselves in a voluptuous confusion of the senses which was in the highest degree equivocal. Though they still found happiness in lying for long periods of idleness on the hot sand of a shelving bank, they were kept, by reading aloud, from approaching too close to one another and revelling in a dangerous dizziness. Jean-Paul, moreover, saw to it that his religious ardour should not cool. He set the young girl crying over some of the more burning and saccharine passages of Lacordaire and Henri Perreyve. Marthe showed a greater liveliness than ever before. She changed the dressing of her hair, and there was a smile in her shadowed eyes when she looked at her cousin. There were certain gestures of hers which once more had that urchin charm which he remembered to have noticed in her when she was a child. . . .

One evening, seated at the piano, she sang Duparc's *Invitation au voyage*. Jean-Paul lay back in an armchair with eyes fast shut. After the final chord, she stayed for a while motionless, facing the keyboard, with her arms hanging loose beside her. They could hear, far off, the guttural cry of a shepherd, and the quick patter of hooves. The grass was gently quivering, but a fresh breeze suddenly made the curtains belly. The gardener was raking the drive. He broke off his work to say to Monsieur Balzon, who happened to be passing: 'Must a'been raining somewhere . . . a'can hear the Saint-Leger bells . . . weather's at set fair, I'm thinking.' Jean-Paul looked at the dim outline of the girl's seated figure. Her head was bent, and her hands looked grey in the gathering dusk. His heart was heavy with a sense of quiet tenderness. He got up, wondering how best he could give her a moment's joy. Then he went to her, fell to his knees, took one of her hands which yielded to his pressure, and raised it to his lips. Marthe made no other movement than that of lifting her head, perhaps to keep the tears from falling. He leaned a little forward, close enough to allow him to touch her dark dress with his forehead.

Then he heard Monsieur Balzon calling for the lamp to be brought, and went out. It was almost dark. The gardener was watering the beds of geraniums and Chinese pinks. The air was filled with a pungent scent of mingled flowers and warm, damp earth.

He reached the road which led to Johanet. Men passing, with jackets flung over their shoulders, gravely wished him good-night. A farm-wagon trundled off into the distance with a sound of intermittent, muffled jolting.

October came. Monsieur Johanet began to make preparations for the pigeon shooting. Every morning Jean-Paul could hear him questioning the gardener from his window: 'Any sign of 'em?'

The young man was dreaming of the future. Ought he not, before marrying Marthe, try to do something for those whom he had led astray? From one of Vincent's letters he had learned that Georges Élie was ill, alone and suffering in a squalid room somewhere in the Plaisance quarter of the city.

'I'll go and see him'—thought Jean-Paul: 'I'll attend to his needs and save him!'

On the last evening of the holidays, Marthe and he set off along the sunset walk. . . . Not a word was exchanged between them. But, moved by a certainty for which they could find no words they felt that they were bound together for life and eternity. . . . The dusk was filled with the cries of shepherds, the barking of dogs, and bursts of laughter. In the bare fields the oxen stood motionless. Young men and women were hastily piling manure into a cart. . . . The wind brought the smell of cow-sheds and burned grass to their nostrils—but it was already mingled with that of damp wood and marshland which persists all winter through on the flooded heaths where men go out with guns in search of woodcock. From far away came the sound of voices calling—'Semero! . . . Semero!'. Other voices from the deep countryside answered them, and, from the fields where the peasants were still at work, from the thresholds of the houses where those who had got home were waiting under the trellis for the evening meal to be ready, the same cry came, telling the guns of an approaching flight: 'Semero! . . . Semero!'

Jean-Paul and Marthe looked up at the sky, in which a crescent moon showed pale.

'The first pigeons . . .' she said.

XXX

JEAN-PAUL plunged into the foggy streets of the Plaisance quarter. Old women dragging carts, were being moved on by the police, with no hope of being able to stop. A man was offering picture postcards for sale, displayed on an open umbrella. The air was heavy with the smell of cooking-fat, pancakes and fritters. Jean-Paul was reminded of a fairground, and thought of the Sundays of marvels and headaches which he had spent on the Place des Quinconces in Bordeaux.

In the Rue Perceval he entered a sordid, poverty-stricken house. The concierge called to him—'Georges Élie?—fifth floor, door on the left.' The stairs were unlighted, and Jean-Paul had to cling to a greasy handrail. He missed the right landing. A thin little girl with yellow hair, appeared in a doorway, and said: 'Are you from the Saint Vincent de Paul?—Georges Élie?—don't know 'im. . . . P'raps he's the young fellow on the next floor up. . . .'

Jean-Paul climbed another flight, and tugged at a dangling string. He heard the sound of coughing, followed by the noise of a chair being pushed back, followed by a shuffle of footsteps . . . then, he saw Georges Élie, with a lamp in his hand, trying to make out who his visitor was. The young workman was in his shirtsleeves with down-at-heels slippers on his feet. A mop of tousled hair concealed his lined and pallid forehead.

'Oh, it's you, is it?'—he muttered in amazement: 'what d'you want?'

'I want to talk to you, Georges. But, first of all go back to bed: I know you're ill. . . .'

Georges Élie shut the door, and slipped between a pair of grimy sheets. He was shaking with cold. A charcoal fire was burning in the grate. Outside the single window stretched the limitless fog which hangs over great cities, pierced, far off, by the lights of a factory. On the table stood two photographs, one of a peasant woman with a Gascon kerchief round her head, who must be Georges' mother; the other of Jérome Servet. The stained wall-paper was covered with notices and proclamations relating to *Amour et Foi*. Beside the bed, under a crucifix, Jean-Paul noticed a view of the port of Bordeaux.

'What d'you want?' repeated the young man roughly.

'It's only natural, Georges, that I should come to see a sick friend.'

'I'm sick right enough. . . . I suppose that with true bourgeois delicacy, you thought it'd be nice to give me the pleasure of a call?'

Thrown out of his stride by the irony in the other's voice, Jean-Paul said nothing.

'I could have done without it, believe *me*. . . . I don't want pity. . . . You remind me of a time I'd rather forget. . . .' In a more muffled tone, he added: '. . . how I've hated you!'

'I have deserved your hatred, Georges. I am cruel and selfish, but, hearing that you were ill, I came . . . because you are still my friend.'

Jean-Paul spoke with the rather shy gentleness, the conscious unconstraint, in which he excelled. His attitude as he leaned above the bed was the one he had always employed in his attempts to overcome resistance.

'You're no friend of mine—not no longer.'

Jean-Paul thought that the note of anger in the other's voice had lessened, but he was tactless enough to add: 'I cannot forgive myself for having caused you suffering.'

Georges jerked himself up on the pillows.

'D'you really think I care a brass farthing for what you feel? All I wanted was never to see you again! So, the fine gentleman really thinks I can't do without him!'

He turned his face to the wall, and said no more. Jean-Paul tried to clasp the hot hand, but it was sharply withdrawn.

The lamp was burning low and making a sooty circle on the ceiling. Jean-Paul turned down the wick. A sudden shower beat at the window, and the equinoctial gale drove the smoke down the chimney. The young man squatted in front of the grate and poked the fire. In a timid voice he asked: 'Is there nothing you want?'

Then, since the sick man spoke no word, he said: 'Goodbye, Georges,' and left the room.

In the darkness of the staircase, which was filled with a stale smell made up of many elements, he tried not to breathe. His heart was dark with gloom, and he thought: 'One can't undo the past. There is no way for me to heal the wound I caused. . . .'

He found himself again in the sordid street where the houses spoke of poverty-stricken lives, of an endless struggle against hunger and sickness. . . . 'I should have given everything'—he told himself. 'I have no longer any right to be happy as the world understands happiness. . . .' He thought of Saint Francis, of the devotion felt by the little brother of Assisi for the Lady Poverty.

'Could I ever be capable of distributing my possessions to the poor?'

As he asked himself, he knew that he passionately loved luxury and comfort. . . .

The crowded pavements of the Rue de la Gaîté lured him on. The harsh lights of theatres and cinemas shone on the pale faces of loafers and thin, sickly children. . . .

He was suddenly filled with a desire to get away from this degraded quarter of the town where even dusk was devoid of beauty. He longed to put on a black tie and short jacket and dine with some well-dressed friend in an expensive restaurant filled with the wild, sad music of a Gypsy orchestra. And, since emotion, with him, always brought to his mind some literary memory he made a momentary denial of his gods: Charles Louis Philippe and Francis Jammes.

Then, he began to walk more slowly. Sad and discouraged, he remembered that Saint-Sulpice would still be open, that there he could find a place for the poverty of his spirit among all the kneeling poverties in the Lady Chapel.

On his knees at a prie-Dieu, he covered his face with his hands, and murmured: 'O Lord, why, after so many efforts, so many tears, am I still nothing but a young man in chains? This evening I have seen, looking at me, the lost eyes of a human soul which, from having known me, has lost something of its virtue. . .

'Oh! the terror of realizing that an act once done can never be undone! Hatred on the face of a young working man has revealed that truth to me. My most shameful deeds are with me still. They press upon me like an escort. I am their prisoner.

'Have I not longed to flee from you, O Lord? With fear I can foresee the sequence of the years ahead—so many afternoons heavy upon my drooping lids, so many nights, abettors of my sins, when the battering shall be tirelessly renewed against my dream of a life of prayer and devotion. . . .'

But when, a little later, he had lit his lamp, he pressed his face to the window in which a scrap of daylight was fast fading. He thought of Marthe: 'I have the great strength of her love. . . .' Then, he brought out her photograph and the most recent of her letters. He looked long and broodingly at those few pages covered with her large and spidery writing, and at the portrait in which she had forced her narrow face into a smile.

Then, silently, he spoke yet other words: 'On that day when my thoughts became centred upon Marthe with a tender and a fixed concern, I began to be delivered from myself. . . .' In the icy little study where the servant had not yet lit the first fire of the season, he found that he wanted to think of nothing but Marthe's smile ever about him, fresh flowers in the vases, and laughter and tears under the net curtains of a cradle.

XXXI

A<small>T</small> that same hour, you, Marthe were sitting on your bed in a large country room. You had not thought to turn up the wick of the oil lamp, and the diminished glow made the mahogany furniture shine. An Autumn rain was running quietly down the window-panes. You could hear in the deep silence of the heath, the bumping of a wagon, the barking of a watch-dog, and, nearer still, the shuffling footsteps of your father, reading as he walked up and down the billiard-room where sun-hats telling of the summer holidays, were hung.

And on the mantelpiece, in the light of the lamp, you had left Jean-Paul's latest letters. Their tender, passionate words had awakened in you the happiness for which you had ceased to hope but which was now to be renewed at every moment of your life—a happiness that made you lie long awake so that you might continue to feel its presence—a happiness that woke you in the night and, in the morning, returned so sharply that, for a moment, you wondered whether it were not the pain of earlier years that was with you still.

But no, that pain has gone. Yet, you know that round your heart, it wanders still and seeks to be admitted. You know that the beloved is, in spite of everything, still that young man in chains who has not yet succeeded in breaking free. . . .

But you, Marthe, smile bravely at all the possible betrayals that lie ahead, absolving them in advance. Your scrupulous love foresees, as its future vengeance, redoubled tenderness and the quiet peace of unspoken pardons.

1909-1912

Printed in the USA
CPSIA information can be obtained
at www.ICGtesting.com
LVHW091135150724
785511LV00001B/173

9 780374 526757